The Mendoza Connection

I0683275

A Lucas Forge Novel
By Scott Sindelar

Paperback Version Published By:
Clean House Press
ISBN 978-1888774078
Copyright © 2014 by Scott Sindelar, PhD
http://drscottsindelarbooks.blogspot.com/

All rights reserved.

No part of this publication may be copied,
reproduced in any format, by any means, electronic
or otherwise, without prior consent from the
copyright owner and publisher of this book.
This is a work of fiction. Many of the characters,
names, places, and events are the product of the
author's imagination or used fictitiously. Any
resemblance to real persons or places is purely
unintentional or coincidental.

1

Dedication

This book is dedicated the best father-in-law a man
could ever have, Richard A Meade.
Thank you for your service to our country, for your
adventurous life, your stories, your support, and
especially for your daughter.

Acknowledgments

A book can be a labor of love, sweat, long nights, and early mornings. Family and friends are often ignored during the process of creation. As a writer, there were times when I was physically with others, but my mind was elsewhere, involved with the cast of characters, plot lines, details, and sudden insights. Please know that I love you and care about you, my family and friends, and I am blessed to have you in my life despite my failings.

This was my first full novel of fiction. I ran into many dead ends and painted myself into seemingly inextricable corners, only to find that my subconscious mind would be working behind the scenes, coming up with solutions.

First, and foremost, I thank my wife, the fascinating and fetching Susan. You put up with too much loneliness during my affair with this book. Still, you continued to support me with your passion and insight. Thank you for making me take long walks in the mornings and reminding me of our love.

I thank my editor, the savvy and insightful Frances Meade. As a fellow writer and lover of books and of the English language, you forced me to think and re-think my story lines and characters. This novel is much better because of your influence.

I thank my long-time friend and fellow adventurer, Brad Lindsay, trike pilot, inventor, creative thinker, and lover of fun and excitement. Your love of Mexico and Pinacate, helped inspire me in so many ways. Check out his website: http://www.savenrg.com

Not least of all, I thank my loving daughter whose transformation into an intelligent, creative, beautiful young woman, has opened my eyes to the world of a new generation.

I wish to thank and acknowledge Front Sight Firearms Training Institute for teaching me the comfort and skill at arms, and for protecting the Constitution of the United States.

To my many mentors and friends throughout the years who have blessed me with your knowledge, insight, and support. Some of you know who you are, and some will remain anonymous for varied reasons. Thank you all.

Table of Contents

Chapter 1   Monday. Lucas Forge- The Call- Arizona

Dr. Lucas Forge was startled awake, the images of his dream ripped away by the insistent ring tone from his cell phone. The room was still dark, vaguely lit by the green LEDs of his alarm clock. Turning his head and blinking his pale blue eyes into focus, he read the dial; 4:07 AM. His phone rang again, triggering a flood of thoughts as his brilliant mind scanned through the possibilities of who would be calling, and why.

Raising his head, he quickly scanned the room. Seeing no movement and nothing out of place, he reached over and tugged at the thin sheet covering his naked body. He slid his muscular legs onto the soft carpet on the floor. He stood up, gaining his balance, and grabbed his phone on top of the rich walnut dresser. Scanning the screen, he saw the foreign area code and the image of a tanned and weathered man wearing a black cowboy hat, and jagged snowcapped mountains in the background. The man in the image was smiling with a full set of brilliant white teeth, but his dark eyes told a different story.

Forge took a deep breath and felt the hairs on the back of his neck stand to attention. Using his index finger, he activated his phone and raised it to his ear, simultaneously scanning the room once more for good measure. With an odd mixture of happiness and dread, he spoke into the phone.

7

"Buenos Fucking Dias, Carlos. Christ, it's 4 AM!"

Forge listened to a few moments of whooshing and static before his old friend Carlos replied.

Speaking with impeccable English, and without a trace of Spanish accent, Carlos retorted, "Well, it's 8 o'clock here in Mendoza, and it's sunny and warm already."

Forge responded with feigned irritation, "Yeah, how nice for you. It's still dark here in Arizona, cabrón."

Forge had heard a rooster crowing in the background behind Carlos' deep baritone voice. His memory brought up an image of the beautiful city of Mendoza. He remembered the kilometers of wide sidewalks filled with tables and chairs and people walking or sitting, drinking rich Argentine coffee. He flashed on a memory of sitting at one of those tables, staring into the deep green eyes of a black haired woman, Alícia. A pang of regret tugged at his heart. His memory was interrupted by Carlos' voice.

"Okay, Lucas. I know what you're thinking, Vato. You're thinking of her, Alícia. I'm sorry, my friend. You never listen to me. You've got to let her go. She's gone and I cannot find her."

"I know. I know," Lucas growled slowly, shaking his head. "Listen, amigo, I'm standing here naked, and it's still 4 AM."

"Ayi, Vato. I love you, hombre, but I don't need that image in my head."

Carlos pushed forward from his leaning position against his old olive drab Land Cruiser. He absently brushed the reddish dust from the back of his jeans. His dark brown eyes focused on the mountains in the distance, to clear his mind of the image of a naked Lucas. He watched a hawk slowly circling in an early morning thermal. The hawk's wingtips were splayed open for maximum lift.

Carlos inhaled deeply through his tanned and crooked nose. The fragrant and warm moist air of the Argentine pampas filled his lungs.

"Lucas," Carlos started slowly, trying to formulate the best way to begin. "There is something down here that you will want to see."

Lucas stared at the wall in front of him. The white paint was glowing a faint green from the alarm clock to his left. His eyes narrowed. He could not help himself, as his trained mind automatically analyzed the tone in Carlos' voice. There was something he heard in his friend's voice: darkness; and beneath the surface, a little fear. Lucas was suddenly fully awake. In the thirty years of their friendship, he had never heard fear in Carlos' voice. Darkness, yes; but not fear. It was neither in his nature, nor in his breeding.

"You still there, Lucas?" Carlos asked, a little softer now.

"I'm here," Lucas replied evenly. "When should I come?"

Carlos looked up at the circling hawk. The thermal was carrying it gently downwind. Carlos felt a fleeting twinge of envy, not only of the hawk's ability to fly, but of its freedom. He answered Lucas's question.

"Yesterday would be fine."

There it was again; Lucas sensed the fear in Carlos' tone. He looked again at the image of Carlos on his phone. The stomach tightened. He thought for a moment about all of the appointments he would have to cancel, but only for a moment. He raised the phone back to his ear.

"I will get started immediately. Buenos Aires or Mendoza?"

The two cities were 1200 kilometers apart. Lucas remembered it was 12 hours by car along the two-lane Nacional Ruta 7, or less than two hours by air. Lucas did not relish a 12 hour, white-knuckle drive with Carlos behind the wheel. If they drove, they would probably make the trip in less than 10 hours, assuming they survived Carlos' maniacal driving.

Carlos thought for a few moments, "Mendoza would be better. I am just outside the city, and I will need to get supplies and find some, uh, cosas especiales. It may take a few days."

Lucas nodded understandingly for both of them, and thought, *cosas especiales, special items, indeed*.

"All right, my friend. I'll text you my itinerary and call you before the final flight to Mendoza from Santiago. I'll see you in a few days."

Carlos whispered, "Vaya con Dios, amigo. Vaya con Dios."

Carlos ended the call and looked up once more for the hawk. It was a tiny speck headed east. Out of habit, a habit that always served him well during his years of military service, he slowly turned around, his eyes scanning the horizon a full 360°. The long mountain chain of the Andes was to the west. The Pampas spread out to the south and to the east. To the north, far behind his Land Cruiser, was a small ranchero in the distance. A wisp of smoke rose from the chimney of the adobe walled hacienda. He stared at the small structure and its cluster of outbuildings for a good minute. Seeing no movement, he walked back to his truck.

Standing next to his truck, he removed a piece of old dried paper from his shirt pocket. Once again, the drawings on the paper puzzled him. Surely it was a map, but what did the symbols mean? Carlos had heard rumors that the local crime syndicate, the one he called the Mendoza Mafia, had been taken over by some mysterious man with mysterious ways. He was supposedly some kind of sorcerer, a Brujo Negro, and he was wealthy and ruthless. He had assassinated many of the mafia Dons and was now also in control of the manufacture and distribution of new, powerful drugs.

Carlos tried to research the Brujos Negros, but could find very little information. He stumbled upon the map in the city library in Bariloche, in a collection of old books. He found it in a book about the Brujos. Trying to make a connection between the ancient Brujos and the modern drug trade proved frustrating. When he questioned some of the street drug dealers, he sometimes heard the name Don Benigno. The men he questioned seemed terrified to even mention that name. *The map must be the key. Lucas might be able to figure it out.*

Carlos' black cotton shirt was becoming even blacker down his back and under his armpits, wet from his sweat. His black cowboy boots were sprinkled with the red dust. Carlos looked thin and wiry, his incredible strength and stamina hidden by the loose cotton shirt and denim jeans. His lanky shape and black cowboy hat made him look taller than he really was.

His rugged and scarred face, and that thousand yard stare, stopped many bar room fights without his having to raise a fist. Patrons often bought him a drink, as offerings of appeasement. His bright toothy smile and quick wit attracted many a señorita, and left behind many broken hearts.

He was partial to the petite natural blonde and blue-eyed Argentine ladies so common in Mendoza, in Barioloche and in parts of Buenos Aires. They could trace their ancestries back to northern Europe when their ancestors fled the war-torn countries during and between the two world wars. Carlos was still amused to hear the musical Argentine Spanish emerge from their pouty Aryan lips. They seemed to swoon at the contrast of his dark muscular skin against their pale flesh.

As Carlos climbed easily into his Land Cruiser, he heard a rooster crow in the distance. It crowed three times.

Chapter 2   Monday-Pinacate Mexico. Jesús Morales – The Fall

Jesús Morales sat down slowly on the black lava boulder. His 80-year-old bones creaked, and a groan erupted from his deeply lined and leathered face.

"Dios mio," he croaked to no one. "I'm getting too old for this."

The old man lifted his straw hat and wiped the red checkered bandana across his sweaty face and neck. He squinted into the setting sun, cursing the heat. He looked down past his white cotton pants, thin and ragged with age and abuse. Despite the calluses on his nearly black feet, he saw tiny rivulets of blood trickling into his torn sandals.

"Pinche burro," he swore.

He had been scrambling for nearly six hours across the Pinacate lava field searching for his lost burro. He shook his leaky canteen. It was almost empty. He realized, too late, that he would never make it back to the shack he called home. The sun was setting over the Sea of Cortez and would be gone within an hour. The mountains of Baja California were like mist in the distance.

"Pinche idiota." He swore at himself this time.

He was never going home. His children might come to his shack next Sunday to check on him, and bring him some tasteless supermarket vegetables, some frijoles, some equally tasteless store-bought tortillas and a case of cheap cervesa. They would find the shack empty and both he and his burro gone. They would panic and spend the rest of the day searching for him and shouting his name. They would not know how to follow his tracks. They had never wanted to learn the old ways.

They would probably drive slowly back to Puerto Penasco, the fishing and tourist port, late in the night, shining their flashlights into the desert, hoping to spot him wandering around. His favorite nieto, or grandson, Enrique, would probably stay behind in the shack waiting for him and drinking his warm beer. Enrique was the curious one. By the time he was 12, he would often steal a car from his parents or his cousins and drive out to his Abuélo's shack in the desert. At night by the fire, Enrique would beg Jesús to tell him stories and teach him the way of the Brujo, the male witch or medicine man.

Jesús swore Enrique to secrecy, because if Enrique's parents ever found out, they would forbid Enrique from ever seeing his Abuélo again. Enrique was a quick learner, but Jesús had forgotten many of the old spells and potions. It had been decades since anyone requested his services. People today preferred to go to la clinica, where nurses and doctors in white coats gave them manufactured pills for manufactured diseases.

Jesús knew many of the diseases they suffered were caused by the growing number of secretive Brujos Negros, practitioners of the forbidden dark arts. The younger Brujos Negros were even experimenting with mixing new chemicals and old potions, sometimes with disastrous results. Many of the younger Brujos Negros did not even believe in the dark forces or the Spiritus Sanctus, the powerful healing force.

Enrique was now 21, and he never revealed the secret training and knowledge he had been receiving from his grandfather. Jesús knew that Enrique's training was incomplete. He felt sad that he might not be able to give him the knowledge that he seemed to crave.

Sitting on that lava boulder, Jesús Morales knew that his end was near. He knew he would never finish Enrique's apprenticeship. Of all his regrets, that was his most painful.

Jesús turned toward the sun. The golden orb was touching the Baja Mountains in the distance. He swallowed the last of his water and flung away his canteen. Facing the sun, he stretched his arms out horizontally, and began the slow intricate dance taught to him by his own grandfather, the last Brujo Blanco in Sonora Mexico. He struggled to remember the words of the lightning chant. His dry throat croaked out the beginning words, but he stumbled and fell onto the sharp rocks beneath his feet.

The old man felt and heard his face smash into the hard lava. He felt a sharp pain in his mouth as the last of his few remaining teeth broke free. The warm sticky taste of iron trickled across his tongue and lips, winding its way into dark rivulets around the tiny chunks of lava beneath his face. He lay there, exhausted, and almost lost consciousness.

Behind his closed eyes, he saw the beautiful face of his Juanita, his bride of 30 years. He saw her as she was when he married her, the 15-year-old girl dancing in the white dress and beautiful veil. It was her quinceañera, the celebration Mexican girls had when they turned 15. He saw her smooth, soft skin when she was 18, when they made sweet love. He saw her face contort and scream out in passion when he brought her to orgasm after orgasm. He saw her face when she was 22 and the mother of their three children. He saw the pain and pride in her face when their last daughter was married. Finally, he saw her broken face and broken body after she was killed by the drunk driver while she was walking on the new highway. She was only 45.

The face of his dead wife vanished and was replaced by that of his grandfather standing next to him, smiling. He saw his grandfather reach over and grasp the hand of Enrique, who was also smiling. Together, they reached down and pulled

Jesús to his feet. They both turned toward the last orange light of the sunset and began the lightning dance. Jesús stood up and followed their movements, feeling a surge of youthful energy flow through his body. He heard their voices singing the chant and he joined in, suddenly remembering all the words.

The three of them danced and chanted for almost 30 minutes. As he reached the end of the chant and his body was contorted into the final pose of the dance, he saw that his grandfather and Enrique had disappeared. He spun around and called out their names.

"Abuélo! Enrique!"

There was no answer. Jesús spun around slowly, but only saw the boulders of lava in the fading light. He looked down at his wet shirt and saw that it was covered in reddish-black blood. He spat out the remaining blood in his mouth. He turned toward the east, and saw the full moon rising. He then turned toward the south, and could make out the outline of the sacred volcano, Pinacate, or Cuk Do'ag in the ancient tongue. The peak rose nearly 1,200 meters above the surrounding desert. He was near its base.

He knew from his studies that the Pinacate is really one huge volcano and 500 smaller volcanoes sitting south of the head of the Sea of Cortez in Mexico. Located mostly in the Mexican state of Sonora, alongside the border adjacent to the U.S. state of Arizona, it is surrounded by the largest active dune field in North America.

The Pinacate peaks lie just north of the fishing resort of Puerto Penasco, or as the gringos called it, Rocky Point. Some believed that the eruption of the volcano coincided with the creation of the Sea of Cortez which followed the San Andreas fault line. NASA sent its astronauts here, from 1965 to 1970, to train for lunar excursions, given the similarity of the terrain to the lunar surface.

The land north of the Pinacate volcano was once a great forest. When the volcano exploded, the forest was incinerated and buried under ash and pebbles of molten rock. Satellite images of the area now show only arid desert and sand dunes. Explorers can find huge pieces of petrified wood inches under the surface of the desert.

Jesús, pulling himself away from his memories, still felt the surging youthful energy roaring through his body. The pain was gone. He felt a force pushing and pulling him toward Pinacate. He began walking slowly; then picking up speed as he reached the base of the volcano. The moon had risen higher, shining its light onto the rocks below. He climbed higher and higher, easily picking his way through the boulders.

When the moon reached its zenith, the white light poured down onto the volcano. He was halfway up the steep slope, when he saw it. There was an outcropping to his right. He saw a flash of light. The moon seemed to be reflected in a circle of rock, polished like a black mirror, at the base of the outcropping.

He scrambled over to the mirror and then suddenly jumped back and turned away in fear. He thought he saw horrible ghost. Creeping forward again, realized it was himself standing there in the hazy reflection. He looked inhuman. Sitting atop his white and bloodstained clothing was the head of a ghoul. His face was mangled and covered in blood and dirt. The mirrored rock was almost a perfect circle two meters across. With the moonlight coming from above and reflected from the mirror, Jesús' body was brightly lit, like an ethereal apparition. Once again, he felt the force pushing and pulling him toward the mirror.

The old, bloodied and broken man reached out and pulled on the left edge of the mirrored rock. It rolled easily, up and to the side, along a smooth groove cut into the base of the outcropping. Behind the mirror was a small round opening. Holding the mirrored rock with one arm, he stepped into the opening. In the moonlight, he could see he was standing on a narrow ledge. Just ahead was a shaft heading downward at an angle. Jesús let go of the circular mirror, and sat down on the ledge, aiming his feet down into the shaft. With a loud thud, the mirrored rock rolled back into place. Without hesitating, Jesús let himself fall into blackness.

Chapter 3 Monday. Arizona. Lucas Forge – The Gathering

Dr. Lucas Forge moved across the room silently and with catlike grace. Suddenly, he heard movement behind him. As he turned, he was body slammed against the wall. With a surge of adrenaline, he spun into a defensive posture as heavy arms grabbed him around his waist. The arms were not skin, but were covered in brown fur.

"Jesus, Bolo!" He growled. "Give me a break."

Lucas looked down into the light brown eyes and grinning snout of his huge dog, Bolo.

"You scared the shit out of me."

Bolo continued grinning, sat down on her rear haunches, wagging her tail vigorously. She was a handsome but intimidating beast. Her fur was a silky smooth brown and her head and muzzle were black. Two light brown patches served as expressive eyebrows. She weighed over 120 pounds. Bolo was a loyal companion, and a great listener.

Lucas knelt down and gave her a big hug while Bolo tried to sneak in kisses with her long wet tongue. He pushed her over and a wrestling match ensued for the next several minutes until Lucas cried out.

"Enough, Bolo. You win."

Bolo continued to stare and wag at him. She could wrestle for hours against her puny human owner.

"I have to go, and you can't come on this trip," Lucas explained.

Bolo closed her mouth and stopped smiling. Tilting her head, her tail wagging slowed.

"Don't give me that look."

Bolo ignored him and put on her best sad dog expression.

Lucas stood up, ignoring Bolo with a twinge of guilt and feeling a chill from the dog saliva on his wet arms and neck.

Flipping a switch, Lucas illuminated the walk-in closet. More out of habit than necessity, he glanced over his shoulder before pressing a hidden release and then sliding open the concealed heavy fireproof door. He stepped inside. Bolo stretched out on the floor of the closet. Pressing another switch, Lucas turned on the bright recessed lights. The secret room was compact, but the walls were populated with recessed cabinets of various sizes, each one meter deep, all securely contained behind stainless steel fireproof cabinet doors. A small workbench took up nearly half of the left wall.

THE MENDOZA CONNECTION

The workbench was a thick slab of hardwood that
Lucas had rescued from a tavern that was being
demolished. He had burnished the top to a mirrored
sheen. On the wall above and behind the workbench
were the tools of a gunsmith, expensive wrenches,
screwdrivers, and dozens of esoteric tools. A
ventilation hood and shaft dropped down from the
ceiling over the workbench.

Nearly one-half of the cabinets contained enough
survival food and water to last for 90 days. One tall
cabinet contained several long guns, including two
Mossberg tactical shotguns, two US made AK-47
rifles, two US made AR-15s with expensive
suppressors and Eotech red dot reticles. The cabinet
also contained a custom sniper rifle. The top of the
cabinet was filled with boxes of ammunition of
various calibers for each of the long guns. The side
wall of the cabinet had containers for dozens of
magazines for the semi-automatic rifles.

A small bookcase contained many volumes ranging
from psychological profiling, theories of
personality, psychopathy, serial killers, and
interrogation techniques. The lower shelf held
books about military tactics and strategy. Several
books in the collection were rare volumes. At the
end of one shelf was a thick manuscript he was
working on; a manual on criminal psychological
analysis and profiling that he was writing as a
surprise for the Director of covert operations. It
could be used in the training of covert agents. Lucas
preferred field work. Imagining the face of the

Director, Lucas thought, *The old man will never get me to take on the passive role of a professor, trapped inside some classroom at the Farm. They can use the manual instead.*

Lucas opened up a middle cabinet door. Pressing a recessed switch, he then lifted the floor panel, setting it on the floor next to his feet. Turning on an overhead light, the muted glow revealed a floor safe. Placing his thumb on the fingerprint reader until a small light turned green, he then spun the dial back and forth until he heard a click, and pulled on the recessed handle. The door of the safe lifted to the right. Surveying the contents, he removed two passports, several bricks of US and Argentine currency, and a handful of small silver coins. Setting these to the side, he closed and locked the safe, and replaced the floor panel.

He stood, closing the cabinet with his bare foot until it clicked shut, and retrieved a black heavy-duty bag from a top cabinet. Scooping the coins into a small bag, he put everything else into a side pocket of the "To-Go" bag. Checking the rest of the contents, he removed the small loaded Springfield XDC compact .45 pistol. The TSA would find no humor in finding the weapon at the airport security check point. He placed the pistol into an empty slot next to the long guns, and shut the cabinet door. It was now 5:00AM.

Retracing his movements, he secured the hidden closet. Taking the TG bag and the small bag of coins with him into the bathroom, he set them on the Italian tiled counter. He pressed a speed dial number on his cell phone for the agency's travel service. It rang several times before the call was answered by a woman's husky voice.

"Good morning, Dr. Forge." She greeted him with a sleepy British accent. "How may I assist you this morning?"

"Good morning, Paula," he returned the greeting, trying to not match her accent. Lucas gave her the proposed itinerary, and added First Class to the request. "Three tickets, please."

"I presume the Director has approved this, unless you have won the Lotto," she chided, knowing they would be paying a premium for the last minute booking.

Lucas smiled wryly. "No, no Lotto this week." The Director would cover the cost, but it would be painful listening to his objections. *Unless I don't return*, offered the small voice in the back of his mind. *Then it won't matter.*

Paula said she would call him back if and when she could make the arrangements. He thanked her and ended the call.

Pressing another number on the speed dial on his phone, he waited until a gruff sleepy voice answered, "What the fuck do you want?"

"Good morning to you too," Lucas smiled.

"Christ, Doc. What time is it?"

"It's time to get moving, Ropes. Carlos called from Mendoza. He found something."

Lucas listened to his friend make groaning noises as Richard "Ropes" Danzinger raised himself to the edge of the bed. Ropes grunted, "It better be good this time."

"Carlos wouldn't call at this hour unless it was. Get your kit together; we're leaving in a few hours. Paula will text you the itinerary."

"Shit, you woke her up too?" He continued, without waiting for a reply, "What about Sparks? He's not tagging along, is he?"

"We need him, but you get to wake him up. That should make your day." Lucas smiled, knowing how much Ropes and Sparks irritated each other.

Ropes complained, "Great, but I'm not sitting next to him on an airplane while he scarfs down those cheesy balls and plays video games the whole way."

Lucas laughed, "You can fight it out on the way to the airport."

"Yeah, we'll play rock, paper, scissors, but I'm bringing a real rock. He cheats."

"Of course he does. That's why he's on the team. He saved your ass last time."

"That's bullshit, Lucas," Ropes whined. "I would have gotten out of there on my own."

"Well, you can sort that out on the plane. Get moving."

"I'm moving. I'm moving," Ropes lied. "I'll call him, although he's probably already awake and surfing porn or breaking into the NSA computers."

"No comment, Ropes. See you soon. Bye." Lucas canceled the call.

He turned on the shower as hot as it would go. While he waited, he checked himself out in the full length mirror. Frowning, he thought, *Not getting any younger*. The hair on his temples was turning gray, but at least he still had a full head of sandy brown hair.

Lucas was never slim and wiry, like Carlos. He had to watch what he ate, and punished his body with regular exercise and martial arts training. Still, at the same height as Carlos, he was 30 pounds heavier. *Must be more muscle,* he mused. The shower was steaming, so he stepped inside, turning the heat down a notch.

Fifteen minutes later, he vigorously dried off, and his cell phone rang. He checked the number on the screen. With a sigh of relief, he answered. It was Paula. The arrangements were made, but she chided him at the cost. "This is way over budget, Dr. Forge."

"No worries," he replied, suddenly cringing. *Crap,* he realized, *That's what the Aussies say, not the British.* Paula laughed anyway. He mused, *I'd like to meet her in person someday.* Thanking her again, he hung up.

Walking back into the closet, he selected comfortable but rugged traveling clothes. Shrugging into his customary black T-shirt, he covered it with a light blue, long sleeved, soft canvas shirt. Pushing the pants hangers back and forth, he finally selected a pair he thought would go with his shirt. He stepped into the light green cotton/poly cargo pants. Pulling his feet into sock liners and then a pair of heavier wicking boot socks, he selected, and then laced up, a pair of comfortable black tactical boots. Frowning, he knew he would have to remove them at airport security several times before reaching Mendoza.

Checking the time on his multifunction watch, and seeing it was 6:30 am, he hesitated, but then thought, *It will go to voicemail.* He punched in the numbers for Tucker, his friend and distant neighbor who lived on a neighboring ranch. As he expected, after four rings, it went to voicemail.

Forge spoke into the recording, "Hey, Tuck. Sorry for the last minute notice. I have to go on a long trip. Can you take care of things up here for me? I'll feed Bolo before I go. You know where everything is." He paused for a moment, thinking to himself, and added, "I'll bring you a souvenir. Thanks buddy. I owe you one. If I don't make it back, Bolo is yours."

Looking at his phone, Lucas decided he had to make one more call. Punching in a number from memory, he waited until the line was answered.

"Hello?" Only one word, and he recognized the voice. "Hello, Catherine. It's Dr. Forge. Is the Director in?"

"One moment, Dr. Forge." Annoying Muzak played in the background. *Really? Muzak?* After a few moments, the phone clicked and a deep baritone voice answered, "Forge? Is that you?"

"Yes, sir. Sorry to disturb you, but there has been a development down South. This could be a break. By the way, according to Sparks, this is a secure line."

"It better be. Don't worry, I have been here since 6 AM. Another break? How do you know there is anything to it?"

"It comes from Carlos. He said he found something. This could be it."

After a long pause, the Director replied, "Standard protocol. We disavow any knowledge of you."

"Understood. I may need some monopoly money in the account."

"Jesus Christ, Forge, of course you do. Unfortunately, I cannot help you with any other, uh necessities or backup. They have the fucking forensic accountants breathing down our neck."

"Thank you, sir, I have some connections for the other, uh, necessities. I'll call you from the sat phone if I have any news."

"Lucas?"

"Yes, sir?"

"Sorry about Alícia. We tried, but came up with bupkis."

"Thank you, sir. That means a lot to me that you tried."

"Anything else?"

"Well, sir, something has been nagging at me. For the first time, I think I detected fear in Carlos' voice."

The Director, steepling his fingers in front of his face, stared through his window. From his fifth floor office at Langley, he had the dubious pleasure of looking out at the water tower and the forest beyond. Lucas' abilities were unparalleled. He had the frightening ability to develop novel strategic and tactical solutions to difficult problems. He could analyze huge amounts of disparate data and see patterns that no one else could see. Even President Reagan once consulted with Lucas, secretly, of course, to develop the policy that eventually caused the USSR to collapse. Lucas was also one of their best assets in the field. Reluctantly, the Director admitted to himself, *Lucas scares the shit out of me sometimes*.

Finally, he responded to Lucas, "If Carlos is afraid, and you are concerned, then this must be worth pursuing. Do you think he got a line on Don Benigno?"

"That was my thinking, sir."

"I don't have to tell you, we really need to get this Don Benigno. The word is, he is taking over the Argentine underworld and moving north into several other Latin American countries. He is the most dangerous enemy we have encountered since Vasili Yurchenko in France. He is making a move to take over the entire drug running operation south of the border. Even the Mexican cartels are afraid of him. In the last month, he's taken out two of our agents, Lucas. One of them I think you knew, Jake Holstein."

The name flooded Lucas with old memories. When he was fresh out of training, Jake and he were in psy-ops together during the fall of the Soviet Union and the aftermath. Jake was older and more brute force, while Lucas was one of the youngest operators. Despite his age, he was able to profile and manipulate the minds of their prey. Lucas invented several new psy-ops techniques that were invaluable to the agency. They both met with President Reagan multiple times. Jake was a good friend who, on more than one occasion, saved Lucas' life.

Looking down sadly, Lucas replied, "I am sorry to hear that, sir, Jake was a good friend. I owed him my life."

Lucas forced the memories of Jake from his mind. The past was over. *We now have more pressing matters to attend to. Jake would understand.*

Lucas said, "Paula has our itinerary, sir."

"I don't want to know any of the details, Lucas. Call me when you have results."

Hanging up the phone, the Director stared into the distance. *Why couldn't we find Alícia for him? Why can't I convince Lucas to start teaching at the Farm? No one has been able to do what he can do with psychological warfare. We need him to train the new agents.*

Grabbing his To-Go duffle bag and a rolling carry-on, Lucas secured his house, set the alarms and hidden cameras. Giving Bolo a goodbye hug, and avoiding her sad eyes, he walked out his front door. Stopping briefly, he scanned the 180 degrees within his field of vision. He listened carefully; nothing. The sun was peeking over the Weaver Mountains to the East. The sky was blue and cloudless, but it was hot outside already. *Well, it's a dry heat,* he smirked.

Rolling his bags down the walkway to the massive structural steel garage/hanger, he stopped at a heavy door and pressed a set of numbers on the keypad. Hearing a click, he heaved open the door. Lucas activated the interior lighting. Standing back a step, he peered inside the immaculate structure. Performing a quick visual scan of the interior perimeter walls and corners, checking the ceiling rafters and heavy beams, his eyes paused briefly on and around each of the several vehicles inside. Breathing in, he inhaled the faint odors; a mixture of diesel, gasoline, and cleaning solution.

Satisfied, he stepped inside, locking the door behind him. He piled his bags inside and climbed into the brown and battered diesel 4WD SUV. He was facing a 100 mile drive to the Phoenix, Sky Harbor airport. If he sped a little, he would make it in time. Pressing the remote to open the garage door, he started his truck before he could change his mind.

Pulling out of the garage, and pressing the remote when he was clear of the door, he checked over his shoulder to make sure the door was closing. As he maneuvered the heavy truck down the long and bumpy dirt road, he gave his ranch one last look in his rear-view mirror.

Chapter 4 Tuesday Evening. Argentina.
Franco Fernández- The Turn

Franco Fernández was shivering under the night sky. His black cotton robe did little to hold in the heat from his naked body. Unable to stand the cold any longer, he carefully stood up and walked over to the pile of mesquite and ironwood behind him. Noticing slight movement in the short bushes at the edge of the plateau, he stared into the eyes of the pair of mules they had used to carry their wood and supplies up the rugged trail. The mules stared back suspiciously.

Franco selected a thick branch and pulled it free, untangling it from the small pile. Turning back toward the fire, he paused. He tried to look, one by one, at the faces of the 11 other men and two women who encircled the fire. Four of the men, facing the fire, had their backs to him, so he could only see the outlines of their heads, silhouetted by the fire light. The others' eyes were closed, but their faces showed the strain of concentration.

Behind him, the moon was sitting eight finger widths above the horizon. *Media noche*, midnight, would arrive within a few hours. A steady breeze from the icy and fast-moving Rio Horcones, bloated from the glacial runoff, added to the chill. Franco tiptoed through the now empty space in the circle and gently placed the branch of mesquite on the fire. He backed up slowly, regaining his place in

35

the circle. The honor of *fire tender* was bestowed upon him by their leader, Don Benigno Sanchez.

Don Benigno, as he was often called, was Franco's mentor and Brujo Superior. Coming up from the barrios of Mendoza, Franco was certain to have led a short life of crime and drugs. Twelve years ago, Don Benigno found him as he was being chased by a gang of thugs. Pulling Franco behind him, Don Benigno faced the thugs on his own, one against five.

The overconfident thugs thought they could tear them both to pieces. Suddenly, Benigno began talking to them in his deep baritone voice. Franco understood the first few sentences, but then Benigno started chanting in some strange tongue and began moving in a graceful dance. The thugs were transfixed. With lightening speed, Benigno sprang upon them like a leopard, breaking bones and sending them to their deaths.

Turning back toward Franco, Benigno was not even breathing heavily, and he stood smiling. Looking into his eyes, Franco was mesmerized by the pale gray orbs that were Benigno's eyes. *Pearls, they look like pearls,* he thought. Franco did not understand what had just happened, but he knew, deep down inside, that he wanted to become a student of Benigno. He wanted that confidence, that skill, that power.

Pulling himself back to the present, Franco glanced to the left to examine the faces of Benigno and the three young men who were previously silhouetted. Their eyes were closed. He briefly looked at the others' faces to make sure their eyes were also still closed.

His eyes then lingered on the beautiful face of Luciana Pillária, sitting across from him. Her long black hair flowed like a turbulent river down to her waist. Her large breasts strained the fabric of her cloak. Her long neck was matched by her long crossed legs that peeked through the bottom of her cloak. Her knees shone in the moonlight and the flickering fire. Franco marveled at her high cheekbones, her narrow straight nose, and her full pink lips. Franco's manhood ached and stirred as he imagined himself kissing those sweet lips.

Suddenly, Luciana's eyes snapped open. Her brilliant green eyes were boring accusingly, right into his eyes. He gasped, and shut his eyes in shame. He tried to concentrate, but her image was burned into his brain. He had lost control, and now Luciana knew it.

Franco counted out the seconds to himself: one minute, two minutes. He then squinted and slowly opened his right eye to see if she was still looking at him. She was not. Franco shut his eyes tightly, and tried to regain his concentration.

Silently, Benigno rose to his feet. He was a mountain of a man, with a huge barrel chest and bulging, muscular arms. His thick black hair fell far below his shoulders. His skin was a walnut brown. But it was his eyes that struck fear into the hearts of everyone. Their color was rare, a gray so pale, that his eyes almost looked like pearls. Many swore that his eyes glowed in the dark. For many, his eyes were the last thing they ever saw, before dying a painful death.

Reaching into the fire, Benigno quietly removed a branch of burning ironwood the size of a baseball bat. He stepped back, and with lightning speed, he swung the flaming branch and slammed it into the side of Franco's head.

Franco screamed in pain as his body rolled out of the circle. He landed on his back, unconscious, but still breathing. Blood flowed down the side of his head saturating the sand beneath him. His body was still, except for his breathing. Benigno stared down at him. No one else dared open their eyes. Shaking his head slowly back and forth, Benigno thought, *Franco, my son. You must learn to suppress the desires of the flesh. You have not learned from my words, so now you must learn from your pain.*

Remembering his own training, Benigno thought once more of the tall and skinny Francesca. It had been many years since he thought of her sweet smile and her hidden ferocity. Benigno had once planned to run away with her and start a life together.

His mentor caught them behind the St. Maria church, her white dress pulled up over her waist, as Benigno was about to enter her. His mentor suddenly appeared and pulled Benigno by his hair, throwing him several meters away. Benigno pleaded with him for forgiveness. Staring into Benigno's young eyes, his mentor unsheathed a long knife and gutted Francesca in front of him.

"Women are born to be sorcerers, Benigno. You must never succumb to their wiles."

Benigno hated his mentor at first, but he soon began to trust no woman. Yet here he was, bringing two women along on this rite of passage. It was as much a trial for him as it was for the women. Long after his mentor was dead, Benigno found ancient texts that spoke of female Brujas. They once existed, but he never met one in all his travels.

Looking down at the unconscious form, Benigno took the still flaming branch and rolled it across Franco's wounded skull, cauterizing the wound. He inhaled the delicious smell of burning flesh and hair. Turning back to the fire he gently returned the branch. He stepped back slowly, and gracefully resuming his sitting position in the circle. He glanced over to the unmoving body of Franco, and then looked over the fire to the face of Luciana. Her eyes were still closed, but he noticed a faint smile across her lips. Benigno stared at her in deep concentration for several minutes before closing his eyes.

An hour later, without the aid of any timepiece, Benigno knew it was media noche. He gracefully rose straight up, without needing to use his arms for balance or leverage. With a deep, resonant voice, he began the malevolent chant taught to him by his great uncle and ancient mentor, the Brujo Negro, Elisandro Sanchez.

Chapter 5   Tuesday. Mendoza, Argentina.
Carlos Cholla – Cosas Especiales

Carlos Cholla turned the wheel of his Land Cruiser and eased the old truck into the parking lot. The lot was peppered with battered pickup trucks, dozens of Ford Fairlane sedans, and a few newer vehicles. He remembered hearing somewhere that the Argentines had purchased all of the old manufacturing forms and dies for the mid 1970s Ford Fairlane. For many years, they churned out tens of thousands of this same model as a cheap mode of transportation for the people.

Carlos glanced at his watch. He had only a few hours before the city would shut down for the afternoon siesta. With his deceptively laconic stride, he made his way into the military surplus store. The interior was dimly lit. He took his time scanning and evaluating the five patrons inside. Three of them looked like Americans in their late 30s. They were examining camping stoves. The other two looked like poor farm workers. Carlos guessed that they worked at one of the many vineyards surrounding Mendoza.

"Cholla! Mi amigo!" The greeting came from the old man behind the rustic and cluttered counter.

Carlos looked over to him, and recognized his old friend, José Montoya. He smiled and waved a hand. "Hola, José. Qué tal? You look great!"

41

He strode over to the counter, reached over, and shook the old man's hand. His grip was like a vise, and Carlos winced. José gave him a big smile with his few remaining and stained teeth. He came around the counter and gave Carlos a big hug. Although he was a full head shorter than Carlos, his hug was far stronger than anyone would expect. Carlos groaned in pain. The three Americans glanced over briefly, mumbled something to each other, and then resumed their shopping.

José spoke to Carlos in Spanish, "It has been a long time, amigo. Are you finally going to move down here to our beautiful city and settle down?"

Carlos smiled, and shook his head. He replied, matching José's native tongue and pronunciation, "I am not old enough to settle down. There are too many women I have not yet met."

José wagged a crooked finger at him, and shook his head knowingly, "Yes, and too many husbands to fight."

Carlos shrugged sheepishly. "How did I know she was married?"

"Well, amigo," José admonished, "you would have seen the ring on her finger, if you were not so busy looking at her breasts."

"Yes," Carlos agreed, shrugging again, feigning helplessness. "I get distracted sometimes."

"Be careful, young Cholla," José warned. "I think her husband is still looking for you."

Carlos exaggerated a look of fear and glanced over his shoulders. José laughed, still shaking his head in mock disapproval.

Studying José's face, Carlos felt a deep love for the old man. He was the father Carlos never had. José and his wife Maria moved here to Mendoza many years ago under mysterious circumstances. José rarely talked to outsiders about his past, but many times over the years, Carlos listened to him talking with Maria on their front porch, reminiscing about their past lives.

Carlos learned that they were born and reared in northern Mexico, but after they found each other, they traveled all over the country. José attended several colleges, but Carlos never learned what he had studied. He did hear José refer to his military training in the Mexican Special Forces, but something had happened and he had to leave the service. They drifted for many years, in different countries, and Carlos heard him sometimes talk about being a mercenary in several wars.

Serious now, and in a conspiratorial tone, José asked, "So, what can I do for you?"
Carlos looked around toward the other patrons before answering. He rattled off his needs, knowing

José could remember even a long list of items without writing them down.

"We need two weeks of outback food, enough for four people, and a multi fuel stove, and some fuel bottles. I'll take a water purifier if you have one." He continued, "Four heavy duty ponchos, some cord, one half-dozen carabiners, one of your *José-especial* first aid kits, four sleeping bags with pads and liners, and," Carlos leaned in and whispered, "500 rounds of .223 hollow points."

José's eyes widened at the last item. He looked over to the other customers to make sure they were not listening. They all appeared to be absorbed in their shopping and their own conversations. His face hardened. "Anything else?"

Carlos leaned back and nodded. "Yes, can you make arrangements for a couple of mules to meet us at Puente Del Inca, near the Horcones trailhead?"

José looked hard into Carlo's eyes. He whispered, "You do not need bullets for hiking in the Horcones Valley."

Carlos returned the hard look. "We may be doing more than hiking. It will be better if that is all you know."

José nodded slowly. "When do you need everything?"

Carlos thought a moment, and replied, "I'll be back in two days; late Thursday. We need to leave here by six in the morning on Friday."

"We?" José asked, with hope in his eyes.

"Not you, José. I need you here. I'm bringing Lucas and the team."

"Lucas?" José's face brightened. "If Lucas is coming, you must first come to my house Thursday night. María will not forgive me if she knows you and Lucas are here and do not come to eat with us."

Carlos smiled. "I was hoping you would ask. Maria makes the best asada south of the Rio Grande."

José replied, "I know, I know," patting his stomach. "Meet me here at 7 o'clock, I will close early."

"Grácias, José. You are too kind, mi amigo."

Carlos turned to leave and almost bumped into one of the Americans, the tall one. He was probably close to six foot five in his cowboy boots. Carlos instantly shifted his weight to the balls of his feet, bending his knees slightly.

"Excuse me, sir," the American began, speaking with a Texas drawl. "You speak English and this Argentine Spanish?"

Carlos' eyes narrowed. He answered cautiously, "Yes." He glanced over at the other two Americans who were staring at him hopefully. They were no threat.

The presumed leader of the group continued, "I was hoping you could talk to the owner for us. We're climbers and need to get some equipment. I want to make sure we get the right gear, but I don't speak this Argentine dialect too good, and I really can't understand it at all when they talk it."

"Did you even *try* speaking with him?" Carlos tilted his head toward José.

The American glanced at José, who appeared to be stifling a laugh. He then answered, "Uh, no."

Carlos shook his head sadly at the American's ignorance. "He probably speaks better English than you do. Not only that, but he also speaks fluent German, Italian, French, Portuguese, and probably Arabic, although I never asked him about Arabic."

The American's face reddened. He looked over at José, who was now chuckling out loud.

José rescued Carlos and spoke to the Americans using a loud voice with Texas drawl, "Hey, y'all, what ken I git fer ya?"

Carlos stepped around the dumbfounded American. As he walked out, and without turning around, he waved a hand to José. Closing the door behind him, he burst out laughing. "Stupid Gringos," he said under his breath.

Climbing into his Land Cruiser, he started it up, and pulled out of the lot, back onto Avenue Juan B Justo, the two-lane road that headed back to Mendoza. A white SUV started up and pulled out after him, hanging back several hundred meters.

Focused on the encounter with the Americans, he failed to notice the four men sitting in the white SUV parked in the back of the parking lot. Never before had Carlos made such a mistake.

Chapter 6   Tuesday. Pinacate, Mexico. Jesús Morales –Inside

Jesús Morales found himself in blackness, falling and sliding slowly down a shaft, with his legs in front of him. He slid almost 10 meters before the incline leveled off and he suddenly stopped. He reached out his hands, trying to get his bearings and to ascertain the size of the shaft. He could only feel the ground underneath him. The air was cool and still. Slowly, he stood up, with his hands reaching upwards. He could touch the ceiling, less than a meter above. He turned around, and looked up, guessing at the direction from which he had fallen. He could not see any light from the top of the shaft.

Turning back, he listened. He could only hear the sound of his heart beating, and the buzzing in his ears. For many years, the buzzing and ringing in his ears were his constant companions. In the silence of the night, especially when he tried to go to sleep, the buzzing sometimes kept him awake. Enrique said it was called it tinnitus. Jesús called it 'Pinche zumbido,' the buzzing of bees.

Ahora que? Jesús thought to himself. *Now what*?

The old man reached inside of his shirt and pulled out a soft leather sack that hung from his neck. He felt inside, fingering several small bottles of different sizes. Choosing one of them, he unscrewed the top. Pouring a small amount of the powdered contents into his left palm, he carefully screwed the top back onto the bottle. Replacing the bottle into the sack, he closed it, and pushed the sack back inside his shirt.

He spit into his left palm, and with the fingers of his right hand, he started rubbing the now dampened powder into his skin. Faster and faster he rubbed. After a minute, he held up his left hand aiming it in front of him. A soft yellow glow emerged from his palm. He smiled to himself, *Well, I still remember some of the old secrets.* In the dim light he could see he was in a tunnel. The walls were smooth and the floor was slightly flattened.

Stepping forward a few meters, Jesús realized that he was now standing at an intersection. He guessed that he had slid down a side shaft, and now was at an entrance to a lava tube, not a man-made tunnel. Pinacate, like many other volcanoes, left these open tubes as the lava cooled. The tube ran to his left and to his right. The left opening seemed to go upwards, while to the right, the opening headed downwards. *It probably goes to the base of the mountain; maybe further,* he thought.

Jesús felt pulled to the left. He aimed his glowing palm to the left and began walking upward. The lava tube was almost 2 meters tall, so he could easily walk without stooping. The air was cool and moist, reminding him that he was parched. *If I don't find water soon, I will die in here.*

He walked a little faster, his eyes adjusting to the darkness. The light from his palm illuminated the path in front of him, but only for several yards. His path steepened and Jesús began breathing heavily. His head began to throb, and his muscles were weakening. He stopped to urinate. He loosened the cord holding up his pants. It took almost 30 seconds to coax his bladder into letting go, and when the urine flowed, he could barely make out the stream. Even in the dim light, he could see the color was very dark, and it smelled rank. His tongue was thick and his lips were cracking and bleeding again. He could taste the iron in his mouth. He shook his head, thinking, *I'm too dehydrated.*

Shaking himself off with his right hand, he pulled up his pants, retying the thin cord around his waist. Jesús took a deep breath through his nose and forged ahead. He began to hallucinate, seeing flashes of light, and his mind wandered back to his younger days. *At least I have lived a good life, an honorable life. I think Juanita would be proud. I think even my abuélo would be proud.*

He tried to remember Juanita's face, but could only bring up a faint image of her outline. His thoughts turned to his Abuélo, remembering a time when Jesús was a young man, barely 20 years old. He remembered sitting in front of his Abuélo, watching him mix and grind various powders in the stone mortéro. Some of the bowls were very old, passed down through the generations.

He insisted that Jesús memorize the ingredients and the recipes. Nothing was ever written down. Jesús suspected that his Abuélo did not know how to write. Jesús, therefore, trained himself to remember long lists of items without needing to write them down. Juanita was so impressed by this, that she often made Jesús show off his memory ability at fiestas and family gatherings.

Abuélo taught Jesús how to find the right plants in the desert and the mountains. He taught him how to track wild animals and birds. He taught Jesús how to fish, and how to dig for alméjas, the large clams that could be found only under the full moon. He taught him the way of the Brujo Blanco. Some of the plants and cacti were unknown, even to the professors at the Universidad.

His mind wandered back further in time, many years ago, when he was a young teenager. Abuélo was asked to come to the Universidad in the city to identify an unusual cactus that one of the students had found on top of a distant mesa. Abuélo and Jesús rode on a dusty bus for two days to get to the campus.

When they arrived, the professor met them at the bus station and drove them to the campus in a huge shiny automobile. The professor pressed a button next to the steering wheel and magically, beautiful music filled the automobile. Jesús clapped and tried to sing along with the music. Abuélo only smiled.

After a long drive, they arrived. Jesús was wide-eyed at the tall buildings and manicured landscape. He marveled at the beautiful and colorful clothing worn by the young men and women walking around the campus. He noticed, however, that some of the students pointed and laughed at Jesús and his Abuélo. He looked at his Abuélo, dressed in his cleanest white rópas and worn sandals. He realized that they looked out of place among all these people in the colorful outfits. He felt ashamed of his Abuélo for the first time. Abuélo, however, seemed to not care. He strode confidently with his head held high.

The professor ushered them into one of the tall buildings. Even though it was very hot outside, it was very cold inside the building. They were in a huge room with almost no furniture. There were colorful banners hanging from the walls. Many people were walking around, although some of them stopped and stared at Jesús. The professor led them to a wall with tall shiny panels, and stopped in front of them.

Suddenly, without anyone touching them, the panels split apart and opened to reveal a small room, also without any furniture. The professor led them inside and the panels closed behind them. Jesús was alarmed and felt trapped. He looked at Abuélo, but he had turned around and was facing the closed panels, calmly staring straight ahead. The professor pushed a tiny button that now glowed. Suddenly, the floor bounced and Jesús felt himself getting heavier. He cried out. The professor turned and looked at him curiously. Abuélo continued staring straight ahead, but put his steadying hand on Jesús' shoulder.

Several moments later, Jesús heard a bell ring and the floor shuddered and bounced again. Jesús felt his weight return to normal. The panels opened and Jesús saw the outside room had somehow changed into a hallway. The professor led them out of the small bouncing room into the hallway and turned right. They followed him for a long way until the professor turned and opened a door to a large room with many high tables with black tops. Several students were standing at the tables and were bent over, their eyes affixed to shiny black cylinders that were, in turn, attached to shiny white metal boxes.

The professor led them to the far corner of the room, where a young man was examining a small cactus lying on a shiny metal tray. He was poking it with metal tools. The professor looked at   Abuélo and pointing to the cactus, he asked, "Do you know what this is?"

Abuélo saw it and became furious. He yelled at the student for desecrating the cactus by removing it from the desert. The student and professor looked shocked and afraid. Abuélo kept cursing at the student, and the professor quickly led them out of the room, back down the hallway, and back into the bouncing room. He pressed another tiny button and suddenly, the room bounced, but this time Jesús felt lighter. The bell rang again and when the doors opened, they were back to the huge room without furniture.

On the way back to the bus station, the professor tried, again and again, to get Abuélo to talk to him, but Abuélo refused to speak. The professor did not make the music play. He even looked at Jesús, as if he was trying to get his help. When they arrived back at the bus station, the professor got out of the car and tried to shake Abuélo's hand, but this was refused. Jesús had never seen his Abuélo so angry and so impolite.

On the long bus trip back, Abuélo spoke gently, but earnestly to Jesús. He said the professor was a fool, and that what he was teaching the students was very wrong, disrespectful to the ways of nature, and was even dangerous. Abuélo was never again asked by the professor for his assistance. Jesús doubted that they would ever return to the Universidad.

Jesús let the memory fade and concentrated on moving forward through the lava tube. The light from his palm was fading and he had to slow down. He was almost unable to keep going, and his eyes played tricks on him, with the flashes of light that were now spinning in front of him. He wanted to stop and sit down, but knew if he did, he would never be able to get up.

He started counting his footsteps, challenging himself to take just ten more, then another ten more, and another. His feet were shuffling now, as he was too weary to pick them up. He stopped and took another deep breath through his nose. Something was different. Sniffing the air, he thought he could detect a faint smell of wood. There was something else. *Leather!*

Pushing himself forward, he noticed that the tube widened. He heard the sound of dripping, but wondered if his ears were now also playing tricks on him. Focusing his last remaining energy, he moved toward the sound. He could no longer see anything, as his palm was no longer emitting any light. He slowly fell to the ground, crawling forward on his hands and knees.

Suddenly, his hands felt a rise in the floor. He moved his hands across it. It felt like a round raised basin against the wall. The dripping was louder now. He reached over the edge, and his fingertips were suddenly wet. He reached in further, and his hands were now submerged into a small pool of cold wetness. Ecstatic, he cupped his hands, raising the fluid to his nose to smell it. It smelled like wet rock. Lowering his cupped hands to his parched lips, he slowly drank. The water was cool and tasted better than anything he ever drank before. He wanted to stick his whole head into the pool and drain it. He knew he had to be careful. He had to let his body slowly absorb the water; otherwise he would just get sick.

Jesús sat down and leaned his body back against the wall next to the basin. He waited several long minutes before drinking a little more water. *Grácias Dios. Grácias.*

Jesús repeated the process of drinking and waiting, drinking and waiting. Even the buzzing in his ears could not keep him awake. He fell into a deep sleep.

Chapter 7   Tuesday. Mendoza. Carlos, the Lion and the Wolf

Carlos drove the short distance from José's store to the Mercado Central. He stopped in briefly to pick up some vegetables and a steak. He also found a reasonably priced bottle of Argentine Malbec wine. The afternoon siesta was about to begin, so he drove back to his room at the Tunkelén apartment-hotel. He appreciated that the flat contained a refrigerator, stove, microwave, and had Wi-Fi, but the Tunkelén also provided maid service and amenities like a hotel.

He parked the Land Cruiser, and while gathering his bags, he did a visual sweep of the parking lot. He saw a young couple, engrossed in conversation, leaving the hotel lobby. There were only a few vehicles parked in the lot. Just as he stepped out of his truck, he noticed a white SUV pulling into the empty space furthest from the lobby. The windows were tinted, so he could not see inside. Carlos spent a few extra minutes, half in and half out of his truck, pretending to be busy with his bags. No one exited the SUV.

Out of habit, Carlos reached to his right hip, where he normally kept his Springfield .40 pistol tucked away, concealed in an IWB holster. While in United States, he never left home without it. Here, in Argentina, however, the penalties for being found carrying a concealed weapon were too severe to risk it. He ramped up his alertness to level orange (potential danger spotted).

He grabbed his bags in his left hand and locked up his vehicle. He touched the hilt of his knife in his right pocket. He walked straight to the lobby, watching the white SUV out of the corner of his eye. It was turned at an angle, so he was unable to see inside the vehicle. Before entering the lobby, he quickly scanned the interior through the glass front door. Antonia was working the front desk. A man was sitting in the only chair in the lobby, hidden behind a newspaper. He was wearing jeans and battered black running shoes.

As he walked into the lobby, Antonia glanced up and beamed a smile toward him. Carlos smiled back and added, "Buenos tardes, Antonia." The man in the chair did not move. Carlos continued walking to the far edge of the front desk, so that he could speak to Antonia while watching the white SUV through the front window.

Antonia returned the greeting in a sing-song voice, "Buenos tardes, Señor Cholla."

They made small talk in Spanish and flirted for a few minutes. Antonia was one of the blond, blue-eyed, petite Argentine women, for whom Carlos had such a weakness. He tried asking her out several times, but until recently, she always coyly refused. The man in the chair never dropped his newspaper, and nothing was happening in the parking lot.

Carlos finally ended the small talk, giving Antonia his best seductive smile and saying, "Well, you know where to find me if you need anything." She gave him a playful shove down the hall, replying, "Buenas *tardes*, Señor Cholla." Carlos shook his head in mock sadness, and walked to his room.

After unlocking the door, he slowly pushed it open. He watched, as the tiny sliver of paper that he had earlier placed inside the door frame, slowly floated to the floor. Entering the room he locked the door behind him. No one was inside. Setting his bags down on the counter, and removing the steak, he put it into the refrigerator. Selecting a beer, and twisting it open he took a long drink and flipped on the air conditioning. Suddenly realizing how tired he was, he sat on the bed and kicked off his boots. *I'm getting too used to these afternoon siestas.* Setting the beer on the nightstand, and pulling down the bed covers, he stretched out on the bed, sinking his head into the pillow. He was thinking of Antonia as he drifted off to sleep.

He was suddenly awakened by the sound of a click. He did not know how long he had been sleeping. In one fluid movement, he was removing his knife from his pocket, snapping it open, and swinging his legs down to the floor. Moving into a fighting stance, he shifted his weight to the balls of his feet.

He stopped, realizing he was looking down the black barrel of a pistol.

The man holding the pistol was dressed in black, with a black bandana covering his face, except for his dark eyes. Neither one moved, except the man was trembling. Carlos sensed the man's trigger finger was slowly increasing the pressure on the trigger. Carlos' heart was pounding. *Never bring a knife to a gunfight*, Carlos remembered.

They both heard the click of his door being opened. A woman screamed and there was the sound of a bottle crashing to the floor. The man in black made the mistake of turning slightly toward the door. Carlos sprang into action. In a flash, he was smashing his left forearm downward onto the man's wrist holding the gun and then grabbed the man's wrist. The gun clattered onto the floor. With his right hand, Carlos brought his knife up to the throat of the now disarmed gunman, while his left hand was twisting the man's wrist and arm behind his back. At the same moment, Carlos swung his right leg behind the gunman's right leg and bent him back, pushing him off balance.

Only then did Carlos look toward his door. Standing wide-eyed, with her hands covering her mouth, and with red wine splattered and dripping down her delicate ankles, was a terrified Antonia.

Carlos smiled at her. "Antonia, I thought you said you got rid of the cockroaches."

Antonia just stared at the two men who were motionless, wrapped together in their deadly tango. Carlos could feel the man trembling even more now.

Carlos locked eyes with Antonia and commanded, "Close the door." When she did not move, he added loudly, "Now."

Antonia jumped at the last command. Without taking her eyes off of the two men, she reached back and shut the door.

Carlos was pulling the man forward and swinging his right foot back around to his side, He growled at his opponent, "Okay, cabrón, back up slowly to the chair."

The man in black followed the order and began slowly backing up. His dark eyes were wide with fear. Sweat was breaking out on his forehead. When the backs of his legs touched the chair, Carlos pushed him down hard, the knife still at the man's throat. Carlos was moving behind the now seated man, continuing to grip the man's right arm behind him. Turning his body, Carlos kept the knife at the man's throat.

"Antonia! Please go over to the table and open my pack."

Antonia was trembling, but did as she was told, stepping carefully over the broken glass and the pool of red wine on the white tiled floor. As she was walking slowly around the two men, she gave them a wide berth. She did not take her eyes off of them while feeling around for the pack on the table. When she found it, she continued moving, backing up and putting the table between her and the two men. Feeling around for the zipper, and finding it, she unzipped the pack.

Carlos was pushing the edge of his blade a little harder against the man's neck, drawing a bit of blood and causing the man to whimper. To Antonia, he said, "That's good. Now reach inside and find the esposas." Carlos thought to himself, *Interesting that esposas means both handcuffs and wives.*

Antonia, without looking, reached inside, searching until her fingers found the cold steel handcuffs. She pulled them out and raised them up. Carlos nodded to her and asked, "Would you be so kind as to bring them here, and come around behind me?" Antonia tilted her head at the confidence and the politeness in his voice.

Walking slowly toward Carlos, she was holding the esposas in front of her. She moved behind him as he had requested. Carlos whispered in the man's ear, "Bring your left arm behind the chair." The man did as he was told.

"Okay, now cuff his wrist, please."

Antonia was fumbling with the mechanisms, sliding the crescent of steel around until it opened up. "So that's how they work," she said nervously. Pacing the crescent around the man's wrist she tightened it until it clicked shut. Carlos glanced at her handiwork and said, "A little tighter, please." Antonia clicked it shut a few more notches. The man let out a yelp.

Carlos unbent the man's right arm and pulled it behind the back of the chair. "Now, the other one, please." Antonia worked the mechanism a little faster this time, clicking it shut around the man's other wrist. Exhaling through pursed lips, she relaxed her shoulders. Carlos smiled at her.

"Bueno. Now, Antonia, please pick up the firearm on the floor, and bring it to me. "

Antonia nodded, and began walking around the men. She continued facing them as she backed around the edge of the bed, until she was standing behind the gun. She knelt down and picked it up. Holding the grip in her right hand with her trigger finger pointed straight alongside the slide, she wrapped the fingers of her left hand over her right fingers. Her right arm was straight and her left arm was bent, with her elbow pointing to the floor. Shifting her weight, she shuffled her left foot until it was pointed toward the handcuffed man. Her right foot was back half a step pointing slightly to the right. Carlos noticed, and was looking at her curiously.

63

Seeing his expression, Antonia shrugged slightly, and said, "My father taught us how to shoot."

"Good to know."

Carlos moved to the side of the intruder, and said to her, "Well then, feel free to shoot him if he moves." Antonia brought the gun level with the man's chest. The man looked at the barrel and then into her eyes. She no longer looked afraid, and was focusing on aligning her sights.

Carlos drew his knife away from the man's throat, leaving behind a thin straight cut, trickling a small amount of blood. He pulled down the man's bandana, revealing his young face. He was barely twenty. The man's nose looked as if it had been broken many times and was never properly repaired. An ugly scar ran from the corner of his mouth and along his left cheek. His mouth was open, revealing crooked and stained teeth. *A mouth breather*, Carlos mused.

Carlos was backing away from the man and was soon standing next to Antonia. He said, "Maybe I should leave the two of you alone." Staring at the man, he growled, "You owe this fine lady a bottle of wine." Looking down at the broken bottle, he added, "An expensive bottle of wine." Turning toward Antonia, he smiled. She finally smiled back, but did not take her eyes off the gun's front sight.

Closing his knife Carlos slid it back into his pocket. "I can take that now," he suggested to Antonia, while reaching for the gun.

Transferring it to Carlos' hands she kept it pointing toward the man's chest. Carlos took the gun and sat on the edge of the bed.

He thought for a moment, and then said, "Antonia, thank you. Maybe you should go now and get cleaned up. I may be here a while, a long while. I'll try to meet you later downstairs, but don't wait up."

Looking at him, Antonia nodded slowly, and started to leave. Stopping, she turned toward the intruder, and gave him a hard slap across his face. The blow was so hard that two of the chair legs lifted off of the floor. Carlos smiled and thought, *You go girl*.

Without looking back, Antonia stepped over the glass and splattered wine, and grabbed a towel from the counter. Bending over from the waist, she slowly dried off her ankles and shapely calves. Carlos felt a stirring in his groin. Straightening up, she looked over her shoulder toward Carlos and smiled. Smiling sheepishly, he watched her leave the room.

Carlos stood up, glaring at the man and said, "Well if I can't have fun with her, I am going to have some fun with you." Sliding the gun under his belt, next to his right hip, and removing his knife, he snapped it open. Pointing it at the man's face, he began moving slowly forward.

The man started begging immediately, "Wait! Wait! What do you want to know?"

Carlos stopped moving but kept the knife pointed in. "It's simple. Why are you here and who sent you?"

The man spoke rapidly. "I am supposed to put a bag over your head and tie your hands together, and then make you come outside and get you into the truck. This is part of my initiation. They didn't tell me anything else. I didn't have any choice."

"They?" Carlos was waving the knife in a small circle in front of the young man's face. "Who are they, and how many of them are in the truck?"

His eyes widening, the man tried to lean away from the knife and kept talking nervously. "There are three others. I don't know the driver; he's younger, like me, but the two in back are older. They are very bad men. The big one they call Lobo."

Chattering on, he blurted rapidly, "This morning we went to a farmacía. Lobo and I went inside. Lobo started yelling at the farmacéutico, demanding a bag of drugs or something. The farmacéutico didn't have it ready. Lobo reached over the counter and grabbed the man's arm and twisted it until it broke. Lobo didn't stop there. He kept twisting the man's arm until the man passed out with pain. Lobo was laughing the whole time. He made me take a bunch of bottles of drugs off of the shelves and put them into a big bag, and we left.

Carlos' eyes were narrowing and he pressed on, asking, "What about the third man?"

"The other man, he is in charge, they call him El León. He doesn't talk to us much; he just talks on the phone and gives orders to us. He is very afraid of and respectful to the man he talks to. I heard him call the man Don Benigno. He told the driver to follow you today, after the farmacía. You obey El León, or Lobo will hurt you." The man was looking even more frightened. "I think Lobo is going to break both of my arms now."

Carlos nodded and thought for a moment. Bringing the knife in closer to the man's face, he whispered, "Well, I'm going to cut out your eyes unless you do exactly as I say."

The man, sweating more, bobbed his head up and down, "Okay, okay."

Carlos asked him, "So, what is your name?"

The man replied, looking down, "I am Javiér,"

Carlos reached over and made the man stand up. Turning the man around, he said, "I'm going to take off the esposas, Javiér. Try anything funny and you will die slowly." Javiér nodded in agreement.

"Now take off your clothes, just your pants and shirt."

Javiér looked over his shoulder at Carlos, and hesitated.

"Just do it, and hurry up," Carlos commanded.

Javiér started quickly unbuttoning his shirt, removing it and setting it on the chair. Bending over, he removed his boots and took off his pants. Standing there in his underwear, he was shivering.

"Now the bandana," Carlos ordered. "Then, face the wall, and don't move."

Removing the gun from his pants, Carlos set it on the bed. Taking off his own clothes, he removed his wallet and slipped into Javiér's damp and odiferous clothing. He switched the wallets. Putting his knife into Javiér's pants front pocket, he found a black cloth bag and a few feet of cord in the other pocket. Tying the bandana around his own face, he almost gagged from the stench of Javiér's halitosis permeating the cloth. Shoving his feet into his boots, he picked up the gun and pointed it at Javiér.

Throwing his own clothes onto the chair he told Javiér to put them on. The man did, without hesitating. Carlos said, "All right, now turn around."

After inspecting the man, Carlos added, "Now put the bag over your head and put on my hat." He tossed the bag and his black cowboy hat over to Javiér, who caught them and slowly slipped them onto his head. "Turn back around with your hands behind your back."

Javiér complied. Carlos reached into his bag and pulled out a large zip tie. Fastening it around the man's wrists, he pulled the zip tight.

"Okay, here's the plan. We are going to walk out to your friends in the parking lot. Keep your head down, and don't say a word. I'll be behind you with the gun, so don't try anything."

Grabbing Javiér by his arm Carlos guided him out the back door. On the way out, he reached into his bag on the bed and grabbed a handful of thick zip ties. Shoving three into his back pocket, he selected three more of them and inserted the points into the slots, making three separate large loops, and then slipped them into his other back pocket. Leaving the room, he guided Javiér around the building to the dark parking lot. Carlos was keeping Javiér's disguised body between himself and the white SUV.

When they were about three meters from the SUV, the rear passenger door started opening and the overhead lights inside blinked on. Carlos saw two men in the rear seat and the driver in front. A very large bald man was stepping out of the vehicle. Carlos assumed it was Lobo.

The big man snarled, "Javiér, what took you so long, idióta? I was just about to come get you."

Raising his empty left hand, Carlos made an exaggerated shrug. As soon as they were a meter from Lobo, Carlos shoved Javiér into him. Lobo and Javiér fell back against the SUV, the black hat flying into the dirt. Carlos stepped back slightly and pointed the gun at Lobo's face. Shouting to the three men, he said, "Nobody move, or Lobo dies first."

Lobo's expression changed in an instant from surprise to fury, but he didn't move. "You are a dead man, Javiér; you too, Cholla."

Sneering at Lobo, Carlos was still pointing the gun in Lobo's face, but keeping his eyes on the other two men. Stepping back, he opened the front door of the SUV with his left hand and said, "Javiér, get into the front seat." Carlos stepped to the side to let Javiér pass and removed the bag from his head. Javiér awkwardly slid inside, his hands still tied behind his back.

Carlos was looking hard into Lobo's furious eyes and said, "Turn around Lobo, place your hands flat on the roof and spread your legs apart. Lobo growled under his breath, but did as he was told.

El León started shifting in his seat. Carlos moved the gun barrel to point in his direction. "I said, nobody move." El León stopped moving and scowled at Carlos, his deep set dark eyes were icy cold.

Searching for weapons, Carlos found a 9mm Glock tucked into a holster on Lobo's right hip, a large knife in a sheath on his left hip, and a spring loaded four-inch blade in his back pocket. Tucking all three into his own pants, he removed Lobo's wallet and found it contained six 100 peso notes, worth about one hundred US dollars, and his driver's license.

Examining the photo, he said to Lobo, "Looks like you used to have hair on that ugly head of yours, Jaime Sanchez."

Lobo turned his head and spat at Carlo's feet.

"Put your hands behind your back, Lobo, I'm sure you know the drill."

Lobo brought his thick, muscular arms down off of the SUV and put them behind his back. Carlos pulled out a looped zip tie and with his left hand; he slid it around Lobo's wrists, pulling it tight until Lobo flinched. Carlos stepped back and said, "Lobo, you and Javiér switch places."

Javiér slid out of the car and Lobo crawled inside the front seat, leaning forward to make room for his thick arms. Carlos said, "Now Javiér, back up towards me." Javiér shuffled backward. Carlos took out his knife and cut the zip tie, freeing Javiér's hands.

"Get in the back, Javiér." Javiér climbed into the back seat. Carlos handed him a long zip tie. "Okay, Lobo, lean back. Javiér, tie his neck to the head rest." Javiér's eyes widened in fear.

Lobo shifted his body, trying to look over the back seat, and growled, "I'm going to kill both of you, and your families too."

Carlos gave him a thin smile, "Yeah, well maybe mañana. Just lean back, Lobo or I'll cut off one of your ears." Lobo snorted, but shifted his body and leaned back. Carlos said, "Do it, Javiér."

Reaching over Lobo's head with the zip tie, Javiér looped it around his neck. Pulling the two ends back around the headrest, he threaded the pointed end through the lock. He pulled it through an inch. "Pull it tight," Carlos commanded. Javiér, shaking and whimpering pulled the free end tight.

Lobo groaned and swore, "Miérda!"

Javiér's hands were shaking even more. The driver stared straight ahead, his hands on the wheel. Carlos pulled Javiér out of the SUV.

Staring at El León, Carlos whispered into Javiér's ear, "It looks like you lost some friends here. I suggest you start running and disappear."

Javiér turned toward Carlos and nodded. Carlos backed up a step and Javiér took off running behind the SUV. Carlos watched him disappear into the night. Bending down, he picked up his hat and slapped it a few times against his thigh to knock off the dirt. He slipped it on his head.

Carlos locked eyes with El León, "Your turn, gatito; Slide over here."

El León bristled at the insult, but slowly slid across the seat toward Carlos. Carlos instructed him, "Get out; keep your hands where I can see them and assume the position."

Stepping out of the car, El León turned around and placed his hands on the side of the SUV. He was much shorter than Lobo, and his fingers barely touched to roof. He was wearing an expensive dark suit and shiny Italian leather shoes. He wore a gold bracelet on his right wrist and Rolex knock-off on his left wrist. His hair was thick, black, and neatly trimmed. His face was clean shaven. Carlos noticed that there was an ugly three inch scar from his right eye down his cheek. *What is it with these thugs and their scars?* Carlos repeated the search, finding only a wallet but no weapons. He tucked the wallet into his front pocket next to Lobo's.

"Drop your arms behind your back," Carlos whispered, and using a looped zip tie, he secured El León's wrists.

El León spat back, "You are so dead, Cholla. I'm going to do you myself. Then Don Benigno will have your whole family killed."

Hearing the name Don Benigno, Carlos hesitated momentarily. Don Benigno Sanchez was the most dangerous man Carlos knew of. He assassinated the heads of many families of organized crime in Argentina, putting himself in charge, and was reputed to be some kind of Brujo Negro. He was thought to be the mastermind behind the new classes of drugs flooding the northern hemisphere.

Shoving El León against the truck, Carlos replied, "Right. You have no teeth and no claws, gatito. You'll have to get in line. Now, get back in the truck and slide over."

El León climbed in and worked his way back to the other side.

Glancing around the parking lot, Carlos confirmed that it was quiet and empty except for a few parked cars. Climbing in after El León, he pulled out the wallet and found the ID. Reading the name, he said flatly, "Leonides Aguilar. Well, Señor Lion Eagle, looks like your wings have just been clipped, too."

Reaching over with his left hand, Carlos felt inside the man's suit coat. He felt something in the left inside pocket and pulled it out. It was a dry and brittle piece of paper. The driver was quietly watching him in the rear view mirror. El León took in a deep breath and let it out, hissing between his unnaturally white teeth.

Carlos carefully unfolded the paper. There was some writing or symbols in a script that Carlos did not recognize. The rest of the paper contained a crudely drawn map. There was a ragged tear on the right edge. Carlos knew instantly that the tear would match the other half of the map he obtained last week. Trying to hide his excitement, he only shrugged and made a noncommittal noise, "harrumph." Carlos casually folded the map and slid it into his shirt pocket.

Pointing his gun at the driver, and poking the barrel into the back of the driver's neck, Carlos said, "Pull up next to my truck."

The driver started the engine, putting it into gear, and drove across the parking lot, stopping next to Carlos' truck. Carlos got out of the SUV, keeping his gun pointed at the driver, and walked around to the driver's door. He opened the door and said to the driver, "Your turn. Get out and turn around."

The driver's hair was long, black and stringy, and was in need of a thorough washing. His clothes also needed a good cleaning. He stank of sweat. Carlos repeated the frisking, finding another Glock 9mm and the driver's wallet. His ID indicated his name was Juan Hernandez. Carlos shoved the third wallet into his already bulging pocket.

Removing his own keys, Carlos handed them to the driver. "Get into my truck and drive. I'll follow you in the SUV."

"Where are we going?" the driver asked, feigning nonchalance.

"Head over to Ruta 40 and go south. Pick up Ruta 7 south and then take it west. Keep going until I flash the headlights, and then pull over to the right," Carlos replied.

Juan, the driver, looked at the keys and then looked at El León. Seeing this, Carlos said, "Don't look at him; he's not in charge anymore. Don't try to lose us, or your boss will get one in the leg."

The driver shrugged and walked slowly to Carlos' truck, taking his stink with him. He looked back once more, before unlocking the door and climbing inside. Carlos moved back to El León's door and opened it. Securing the gun in the small of his back, behind his belt, he took out another long zip tie and quickly wrapped it around El León's neck and the head rest. El León started struggling until Carlos punched him hard in the ribs. El León coughed and sputtered. Carlos slammed El León's head back into the head rest, and pulled the zip tie tight, trapping El León's head and neck.

Slamming the door shut, Carlos got into the driver's seat of the SUV. Lobo struggled a little, but his face turned red when he realized he was just choking himself against the zip tie around his neck. Carlos ignored him, removing the gun from behind his back, and slipping it under his right thigh. He shifted the SUV into reverse, and backed up five meters. He waited while Juan started the truck and began driving out of the Tunkelén parking lot. Carlos followed closely behind him.

Winding around the side streets for several blocks, Juan found the entrance to Ruta 40 and turned right. Carlos frequently checked his rear view mirror to glance at El León, and to check if they were being followed. El León glared back, using his eyes like daggers.

Lobo started cursing at Carlos, defaming his parentage and explaining what he was going to do to various parts of Carlos' body. Spittle was flying out of his mouth during this tirade. Carlos let him vent like that for a few minutes, until Lobo started repeating himself. Removing his gun from under his thigh, Carlos pointed it at Lobo's face. In a menacing tone, he said, "Shut the fuck up already, Lobo. Your limited command of the Spanish language is giving me a headache." Lobo closed his mouth, but his eyes were bulging with hatred. Carlos replaced the gun under his thigh.

They drove for almost an hour up the winding road, gaining elevation up into the mountains. Soon, Carlos could see the dark waters of the Potrerillos Reservoir on the right. He spotted the overlook and flashed his lights at Juan, the driver. Juan pulled over and Carlos pulled up alongside. Jumping out, Carlos pointed the gun at Juan. "Get out, now," Carlos insisted. "Leave my truck running."

Crawling out of the truck, Juan stood looking confused. Carlos pointed at the SUV and said, "Move over to the side of the SUV."

Juan was staring at Carlos, still confused, but he complied and moved to the side of the SUV. Carlos continued, "Turn around and put your hands behind your back."

Juan started to protest, his eyes pleading and tearing. He pushed his palms together, as if praying. "Please, please señor, I'm only the driver," he cried.

Carlos snorted, "Yeah, only the driver with a 9 millimeter and a Mendoza Mafia tattoo on your neck. Turn around."

Juan slowly reached up with his right hand and rubbed the tattoo on the side of his neck. He was trembling now, but turned around. Slowly he moved his arms around behind him. Removing the third looped zip tie, Carlos used it to secure Juan's wrists. "Get in back," he ordered.

Carlos opened the side door and Juan crawled in next to El León. Carlos used the last zip tie to secure Juan's neck to the head rest. All three men started yelling and cursing. El León was kicking the seat in front of him.

Carlos closed the door and walked slowly around to the driver's side door, looking down at the ground. Seeing what he was looking for, a large rock, he tucked the gun into the small of his back, bending down, he picked up the rock using both hands.

Waddling over to the front seat, Carlos dropped the rock onto the floorboard with a loud thump. Taking a few seconds to look into the screaming faces of each of the three men, Carlos bent down and shoved the rock onto the accelerator pedal. The engine roared. He aimed the front wheels toward the edge of the overlook. Slamming the SUV into gear, and jumping back, Carlos watched as the vehicle lurched forward, picking up speed. The men were screaming louder. Hitting the curb, the front of the SUV bounced up and flew over the edge of the cliff, going airborne and slowing rotating downward. The screams were fading as the truck rocked downward.

Carlos ran to the edge just in time to see the SUV slamming into the water far below. The lights of the SUV kept burning, as vehicle rapidly sank below the surface. Carlos continued watching until the lights dimmed and then went out. Unconsciously, Carlos made the sign of the cross.

Driving back to the hotel, Carlos felt uneasy, and his mind tried to sort out the recent events. *How did they find me? Do they know about José and how he has helped me? This fucking Don Benigno seems to be involved in everything. Why the hell am I feeling afraid?*

Pulling into the hotel parking lot, Carlos turned off the engine and sat quietly. It always took him an hour or more to decompress after being involved in wet work. He truly believed he could compartmentalize and suppress the ugly parts of his work. If he didn't believe that, he would be unable to go on. He might end up like his fellow soldiers that disappeared from the world and ended up secluding themselves in some wilderness or desert, far from civilization.

Reassuring himself, he thought, *They were evil men, working for an evil boss. I had to do what I did.*

Pulling himself together, Carlos left his truck, walking back toward the hotel lobby. The lights were still on, but the lobby was empty, except for Antonia, who was typing something into her computer.

Opening the door and stepping inside, he saw Antonia jump away from her computer with a look of fear on her face. In a millisecond, she recognized Carlos and ran toward him.

Rushing into his arms, she almost collapsed. Holding each other silently for almost a minute, Antonia leaned back, looking into his eyes.

Suddenly she blurted out a series of questions. "Dios mio, Carlos. What was that all about? Are you okay? Who was that man? Are you okay? Is he coming back?"

Unable to help himself, Carlos started laughing uncontrollably. "Slow down, Antonia. We are fine. I took care of him." Looking deeply into her eyes, he added, "You have nothing to worry about."

"Who was he?"

Looking away, Carlos replied, "He was just some idiota who had the wrong man. I set him straight, and sent him on his way. I guess he thought I was someone else."

"Weren't you afraid? He had a gun!"

"Well, he had a gun for a few seconds. Then he didn't have a gun. Then you had the gun. By the way, you were awesome!"

Blushing, Antonia thought back to the events earlier in the evening. "Yes, we both were awesome." A few moments later, she asked, "What really happened to him?

"I took him outside, scared the shit out of him, and he ran away."

Staring into his eyes, she reached up and pulled his head toward her face. Keeping her eyes open, she kissed him. He kissed her back, pulling her tightly against him.

"When do you get off work?" he whispered.

"The office is now closed."

Chapter 8   Wednesday. Santiago de Chile

Lucas Forge was startled awake by the annoyingly loud flight attendant announcing the impending landing at Santiago de Chile. The flight attendant's voice was blaring over the speakers in Spanish and then she repeated her monologue in English. Lucas covered his ears to dampen the high decibel announcement.

When she finished, he checked his watch. It was almost 6 AM. He had been flying, or had been in airports, for almost 24 hours. Although he was in premium business class, his muscles felt stiff. Looking out the window of the Boeing 787, he saw it was still dark. Sunrise was still two hours ahead.

Looking over to his right he could see Ropes was snoring. Ropes had inserted earplugs and then covered his ears with noise cancelling headphones, so he slept through the announcement.

Ropes was the shortest in the group and he was bowlegged and wiry. The veins and muscles in his arms were highly defined. His arms seemed longer than they should be, and this, plus his disheveled red hair and beard made him look like a skinny orangutan.

Craning his neck, Lucas looked back over the seats to see Sparks furiously tapping on his laptop, earphones jammed into his ears. Sparks was the tallest and thinnest member of the team, and the least athletic. His diet was horrible, consisting of energy drinks, cinnamon candies, and salty snacks. No one had better get between him and a bag of Fritos. Somehow, he was able to eat enormous meals without gaining an ounce.

He didn't hear the announcement either, Lucas concluded. Smiling to himself, Lucas knew what was going to happen soon.

A few minutes later, the loud-mouthed flight attendant was shaking Sparks' shoulder, telling him to turn off his electronics. Sparks jumped at her touch, and pulled out his earphones. Looking around, disoriented, he sighed and shut down his laptop. Crossing his arms, he scowled, looking miserable without his computer.

Ten minutes later, the Boeing hit hard on the airstrip and bounced. Startled awake, Ropes lurched upwards, arms and fists clenched in a fighting stance, but he was restrained by his seatbelt. Lucas burst into laughter at the flailing monkey-man. Glaring at him, Ropes punched Lucas in the shoulder. Lucas continued laughing, and, like a kid in church, he couldn't stop.

"Welcome to Santiago," he snorted.

"Fuck you, Doc," Ropes was shouting, his ears still plugged and unable to hear the volume of his own voice. He craned his neck around toward Sparks, who quickly looked out the window, his hand covering his grinning face.

They had a three hour layover in Santiago, and had to switch gates and planes. Ropes hurried off in search of a coffee bar while Sparks hunted down an electrical outlet to recharge his laptop. Lucas flirted with one of the pretty dark-haired flight attendants at the new gate. His interest increased when she told him she lived in Mendoza, and would be getting off their plane when it landed. Sparks was watching him enviously, but pretended to be absorbed by his computer. Soon, he forgot about them as he found something more interesting online.

Ropes came back with three cups of coffee and a bag of Chilean Cheese balls that he threw onto Sparks' keyboard. Sparks jumped, but then looked up at Ropes in surprise. Ropes handed a coffee to Lucas and one to Sparks, who was looking at him suspiciously.

"Why are you being nice to me?" Sparks asked.

Ropes glared at him and replied, "To keep you quiet, egghead."

"Uh, thanks, Ropes. That's the nicest thing you've ever done."

"Yeah, well, you owe me now," Ropes growled.

Sparks started to answer, but Ropes held up his hand, and glared at him, shaking his head.

Raising his cup as a thank you, Sparks set the cheese balls aside. Looking back at his laptop he started sipping the coffee. *Hmmm, cream and four sugars. How did he know?* Looking over his steaming cup, Sparks studied Ropes' bowlegs as he ambled across the waiting area and took a seat with his back to the windows.

Reaching into his carry-on bag, Ropes pulled out a pair of dark sunglasses and an olive drab ball cap. Sliding the sunglasses over his eyes, he slipped the cap over his thick red hair. Pulling down on the cap's brim, he was pretending to sleep, while secretly watching the people scurrying around the waiting area.

Lucas and the flight attendant were still flirting with each other, when at 10:30 am, another overly loud woman's voice started blaring over the intercom.

"LAN airlines flight 931 from Santiago Chile to Mendoza Argentina is now boarding at Gate 3."

The pretty flight attendant's face started reddening as she realized she had been shirking her duties while being mesmerized by Lucas' charm. Slipping him her card, she turned and hurried toward the gate. The gate attendant gave her a disapproving look, which was in contrast to the decidedly approving looks from the three Americans.

Standing in line, Lucas whispered to his companions, "It is a short one hour flight. We will get there in time for lunch." Pushing buttons on his cell phone, he sent a text to Carlos.

Moments later, his cell phone was vibrating. Looking at the screen, Lucas' face darkened. Carlos had replied with two letters, "TC." Translating in his mind, Lucas knew what it meant: *Ten cuidado – be careful.*

Glancing around to make sure no one was watching except his two friends, Lucas signaled to them using subtle finger movements. They both signaled back, *Understood.*

Many years ago, Lucas developed a secret sign language using minimal finger and hand movements. These were sometimes accented by leg, foot and body positions. As a team, they developed this large private vocabulary system for silent and nearly imperceptible secret communication. It took years of practice, but now they could carry on a verbal conversation while at the same time communicating complex information rapidly using their non-verbal channel.

Pretending to chat out loud about the vineyards in Mendoza, the three were actually making strategic plans for handling the potential scenarios awaiting them in Mendoza and beyond.

Chapter 9   Wednesday. Argentina. Franco Fernández - Pain

The pain was almost unbearable. A part of Franco's mind was pulling him downward, back into the soothing bliss of painless unconsciousness. The other part of his mind, his life force, was fighting against the downward pull, dragging him upward into awareness. With each beat of his heart, lightning bolts of intense hot pain seared across his brain. The cold breeze, licking the left side of his face, only exacerbated the raw burning pain emanating from his cheek and temple.

Opening his eyes, he saw only dancing dots of flashing lights in front of the darkness beyond, pulsing with each heartbeat. Closing his eyes and inhaling deeply, the acrid odor of burnt hair and flesh infused his nostrils. Franco lay on his side, unmoving, sensing the sharp stones digging into his right cheek and ear.

Consciousness was winning a Pyrrhic victory over the seductive pull of nothingness. Franco's Brujo Negro training bumped and lurched into operation. Holding his breath, he began listening intently for any sounds of movement or impending danger. Hearing only the soft sound of the wind and the rushing water of the Rio Horcones, he exhaled slowly, pushing toxic air from inside his lungs out through the small opening he formed with his pursed lips. Inhaling deeply through his nose once again, he forced his olfactory sense to separate out the burnt skin smell, focusing on the rest of the odors.

He was now making out the different scents. One by one, he identified them individually. *Sweet mesquite smoke, pampas grass, lava stones, bitter ironwood smoke, limestone, moldering beavertail cactus, mule dung, wet sand, the hallucinogenic colubrina beans, aloe,* and something else.

What is that odor? Franco Fernández searched his memory, images coming into his mind. He was seeing the line of black robed figures, hiking up a steep trail. In front of him, a figure was moving just a few meters ahead. *Yes. That was it; the unmistakable aroma of Luciana Pillária. Why do I smell her now?*

Slowly opening his eyes, Franco tried peering past the still flashing lights behind his eyes, and into the darkness. Without moving his head, he could make out swirling wisps of smoke and the flickering coals of the fire pit. Strands of pampas grass were swaying in the breeze. The ground was glowing from the light of the full moon and shadows from a scrubby mesquite were lengthening almost imperceptibly. *How long have I been out?*

Looking upward, something was blocking his vision. Then he felt it, something wet and heavy on the side of his burning face.

Remaining motionless except for his rhythmical breathing, Franco took a mental inventory of the rest of his body. Starting with his feet, he could feel the tight sandals and gritty dirt between his toes. Sharp rocks were digging into his calf, thigh and hip. No other pain was signaling any injury. His stomach felt queasy and gurgled with slow internal movements. His breathing felt full, painless, and sounded clear. His right shoulder was sore and his arm was trapped beneath his chest. Looking down, he found his hand, palm up, and fingers peeking out from under his robe. Moving each finger of his right hand, he concluded that nothing was broken or cut.

Focusing on his left arm, Franco noted he felt no pain, and his fingers moved freely. Drawing his left hand up to his face, he felt the rough ridges of the thing that was covering his wound. Touching it sent a sharp pain across his face and temple.

Deciding that he had nothing to lose, in one swift movement, Franco drew his legs up under him and pushed himself into a crouching position. His head exploded in pain, blinding him with a burst of flashing lights behind his eyes. Forcing his eyes to remain open, he quickly looked around him in all directions. His arms were raised in a defensive fighting position. Everyone was gone, including the mules. He was alone.

The thing on his face peeled off and fell on the ground in front of him. The cold breeze slapped his face, the frigid air both cooling and accentuating the burning. Looking down, Franco identified the wet objects lying on the ground. They were strips of aloe vera, sliced open. A little to his right several uncut strips of aloe vera were lying on a small ribbon of white cloth. A crudely drawn arrow on the cloth was pointing to the west.

Looking up and following the arrow, Franco squinted into the distance. Rising up from the horizon was Tupungatito, the Little Star Viewpoint volcano. In front of it, and to the left, was its mother, the massive Tupungato volcano. Tupungatito last erupted more than thirty years ago, before Franco was born, but it was still considered active.

Tupungatito rose nearly 6,000 meters above sea level. *Surely they are not going to the summit,* Franco thought. He tried to remember the cryptic conversations they had with Benigno. Benigno mentioned something about a doorway, but that made no sense. As far as Franco knew, there were no houses or buildings this far into the mountains.

During the short time he had before leaving for this journey, Franco had done a little research. He remembered reading about the mysterious crash of an airliner soon after the end of World War II. He forced his mind to recall the details.

On August 2, 1947, the airplane Star Dust was carrying six passengers and five crew members, when it crashed into a steep glacier high on the

Argentine side of Tupungato. The plane burned and an avalanche buried the wreckage. The plane lay undetected, deep beneath the snow and glacial ice for over 50 years before its remains finally re-emerged at the glacier terminus.

In 1998, two Argentine mountaineers climbing Cerro Tupungato found the wreckage of a Rolls-Royce Merlin aircraft engine. They also found twisted pieces of metal and shreds of clothing in the Tupungato glacier at an elevation of almost 5,000 meters. In 2000, an Argentine army expedition discovered more scattered debris and wreckage, collecting some of the evidence for investigation.

Speculation included theories of international intrigue, corporate sabotage, and even abduction by aliens. The last word in Star Dust's final Morse code transmission to Santiago airport was STENDEC. It was received by the airport control tower four minutes prior to the planned landing, and the same message was repeated twice. It has never been satisfactorily explained.

The Star Dust's captain, Reginald Cook, was an experienced Royal Air Force pilot with combat experience during World War II. His first officer, Norman Hilton Cook, and second officer, Donald Checklin also had combat experience. Captain Reginald Cook had been awarded the Distinguished Service Order and the Distinguished Flying Cross medals. The radio operator, Dennis Harmer, also had a record of wartime service. The crew also included Iris Evans, a flight attendant or "Stargirl", who previously served in the WRENS, the Women's Royal Naval Service.

The six passengers were Casis Said Atalah, a Palestinian, returning home to Chile from a visit to his dying mother; three businessmen Jack Gooderham, Harald Pagh, and Peter Young; Paul Simpson, a British civil servant, and Marta Limpert, a Chilean resident of German origin. Atalah is said to have had a diamond with him (stitched into the lining of his suit). Simpson was functioning as a King's Messenger, with secret diplomatic documents destined for the British embassy in Santiago.

A report by an amateur radio operator, who claimed to have received a faint SOS signal from Star Dust, initially raised hopes that there might have been survivors. All subsequent attempts to find the vanished flight over the years failed.

There was speculation that the flight might have been blown up in order to destroy the diplomatic documents being carried by passenger Paul Simpson. Others suggested that Star Dust might have been taken or destroyed by a UFO, an idea fueled by unresolved questions about the flight's final Morse code message. Later, two other aircraft, also belonging to British South American Airways, mysteriously disappeared.

Shivering, Franco turned away from the volcanoes and their mysteries. Unsheathing his long knife from his belt, he knelt down and sliced open one of the aloe vera leaves. Carefully placing the wet sides against his face, he wrapped the cloth ribbon around his head to hold them in place against his raw flesh.

Grabbing the remaining branches of Mesquite and Ironwood, he placed them in the fire pit, coaxing the fire back to life. Sitting down in front of the warming flames, Franco closed his eyes and began reciting the *Cantar Doler*, the chant against pain.

> *Pain is the enemy*
> *I will not feel it*
> *Pain is the distracter*
> *I will not acknowledge it*
> *Pain is an illusion*
> *I will not believe it*
>
> *Pain is passing through me*
> *It is draining into the ground*
> *beneath my feet*
> *Pain is no longer part of me*
> *As I step away, I will leave my pain*
> *behind me*
> *It no longer exists within me*
> *The pain lives only in my footprints*
> *And I am now free*

Again and again, Franco sang this song to himself. Opening his eyes, he saw the fire had almost consumed itself. Placing the remaining strips of aloe vera into a side pocket of his small backpack, he stood up. Stepping away from the fire, he looked up toward Tupungatito, and began walking toward it. Sniffing the air, he convinced himself he could smell the scent of Luciana Pillária. His pain remained behind in his footprints.

Chapter 10 Wednesday. Mexico. Jesús Morales - Deeper

Jesús began stirring out of his deep slumber. Opening his eyes made no difference, there was only blackness. The sound of dripping water was behind him, and he rolled over, remembering the basin of water that saved his life. Reaching out in front of him, he crawled toward the sound, until his hands touched the edge of the basin. Still thirsty, he drank handfuls of water, renewing his energy.

Sitting up, Jesús began his morning ritual. It was the discipline taught to him by his Abuélo.

> *Thank you for my feet and all my toes.*
> *I am blessed.*
> *Thank you for my legs.*
> *I am blessed.*
> *Thank you for my manhood.*
> *I am blessed.*
> *Thank you for my working bowels.*
> *I am blessed.*
> *Thank you for my hands and all my fingers.*
> *I am blessed.*
> *Thank you for my arms and shoulders.*
> *I am blessed.*
> *Thank you for all my senses.*
> *I am blessed.*
> *Thank you for my mind.*
> *I am blessed.*
> *I am a blessed man and I am grateful.*

He added one more:
Thank you for the water that quenches my thirst.
I am truly blessed.

Jesús reached inside his shirt for his pouch. Finding the bottle, he unscrewed the top and tapped more of the powder into his left palm. Carefully returning the bottle to his pouch, he spit into his palm and began rubbing furiously until the yellow glow emerged. Aiming the glow in front of him, he saw the basin and a trickle of water dripping from a protruding rock hanging above it. *I wish I had kept my canteen, and not let my anger make me throw it away*, he thought.

Turning around slowly, he squinted into the darkness, seeing nothing in front of him. Raising his palm upward, he was able to find the roof of the tunnel almost one meter above him. Turning to the right, he continued walking upward through the tunnel. Within a few seconds, he began to see the outline of a boulder with a flattened top, like a small mesa. "Dios mio," he exclaimed. The top of the boulder was covered with many objects.

Aiming the glow toward the top of the boulder, he saw three small bottles, two large bottles, a small wooden box, a thick leather book, a small metal bowl, and an ornate leather belt with a long leather scabbard containing what appeared to be some type of sword. The guard of the sword glinted in the yellow glow, and the hilt appeared to be wrapped in greasy leather. Next to the sword were several thick candles, and a round metal container with a small gnarled knob near the top. Fitted to the top of the container was a glass globe, opening at the top. "Eso es un fanal de aceite," (It is an oil lamp), Jesús exclaimed out loud.

Reaching for the box, Jesús unfastened the clasp and lifted the lid. Inside the box were a 10 cm long cylinder and a metallic blade. *Dios mio! Espero eso es un pedernal.* Reaching inside the box, he removed the two items and scratched the blade along the flint cylinder. Sparks scattered onto the top of the boulder, almost blinding him with their light. Jesús began jumping and dancing in circles, looking upward. "Grácias! Grácias!" he exclaimed.

Using the glow from his palm, he found the oil lamp. Unscrewing the knob on the side of the base, Jesús shook the container gently. He heard and felt liquid sloshing inside. Lifting the container to his nose, he smelled inside the opening. *Aceite* (oil). Closing the knob, he removed the glass globe, setting it on the top of the mesa. Turning the lamp over, he shook it several times to wet the wick emerging from the top of the base of the lamp. He felt around the mesa and found the cylinder and blade. Scraping the cylinder several times, sparks flew and he finally inflamed the wick. It flickered slowly and dimly, and then began to burn brightly. Jesús slipped the globe into the fittings on top of the metal base. His eyes were watering from the sudden brilliance.

Looking around, he lifted the lamp and he saw he was in a small room. The lamp was lighting the whole area with a bright yellow glow. The water basin was actually recessed into the wall of the tunnel. Against the opposite wall was a wooden chest.

Feeling both confident and curious, Jesús shuffled over to the chest. Hesitating only a few seconds, he reached down and opened the lid slowly. The metal hinges creaked and the sound echoed off the walls of the tunnel. Inside the chest, on the left, was a neatly folded pile of white cloth. In the middle, there were several wooden boxes that appeared to be sealed with wax. On the right, there were several pairs of leather sandals with thick soles. They were sitting on top of a leather pack.

Reaching inside the wooden chest, Jesús lifted the cloth. Setting the lamp on the floor, he used both hands to shake out the cloth. Holding it in front of him, he saw that it was a long thick robe, with long sleeves and a hood. Suddenly realizing how cold he was inside this tunnel, Jesús wriggled his body into the robe. The long sleeves had cords at the end so that he could tighten them around his wrists. The bottom of the robe fell to the tops of his ankles.

Looking down his blood-soaked sandals, Jesús knelt down and removed them. He walked barefoot across the cold floor to the water basin. Scooping water out of the basin, he cleaned his feet with the cool liquid. Dark rivulets of fluid were snaking down the tunnel. Remembering the bottles on the mesa, he walked over to it, leaving wet and bloody footprints behind him. He opened the first large bottle and sniffed the contents. Aceite, more oil for the lamp. He opened the second large bottle and sniffed the contents, pulling his face back quickly at the sharp smell. *Mescal!* He smiled, recognizing the fermented agave contents. Holding the bottle in front of him, he swirled it around until he saw the agave worm floating on the bottom.

Smiling broadly, he reasoned, *Well, one sip won't hurt, and I need to sterilize my mouth.* Lifting the bottle to his lips, Jesús took in a large mouthful. He let the mescal sting his lips, broken teeth and gums, swishing it around before swallowing. Coughing and sputtering, he grimaced. The liquid burned his throat and he could feel it hit his empty stomach like a blow torch. Steadying himself with one hand on the mesa, he set the bottle down and re-sealed it with the cork.

Standing upright suddenly, he looked around, frowning, and wondered, *Who left all of this here? Why, and when are they coming back?*

Looking back down at the mesa, he saw a small gray rectangular block. Picking it up, he brought it to his nose and sniffed. It smelled vaguely of sandalwood and rose. He carried it back to the water basin. Splashing some water on it, he rubbed it with his fingers. *It is soap*, he realized.

Despite the cold, he climbed out of his robe and his clothing, and set them on the mesa. Picking up the small metal bowl, he walked back to the water basin. For the next several minutes, he poured water over himself, screaming out loud at the cold, and using the soap to clean himself from head to foot. Using his old clothing to dry himself off, he finally slipped into the thick robe. He started to move back to the chest, but decided to take *uno mas,* one more small sip from the bottle of mescal. His mouth still burned, but a little less this time. The fiery liquid coursed its way into his stomach. Now feeling woozy, he sealed the bottle and shuffled back to the chest.

Selecting sandals that would fit his feet, he plopped down next to the chest. *Dios mio, estoy borracho.* Leaning on the trunk, he held his head in his hand until the dizziness passed. Lifting one of the wooden boxes out of the trunk, he examined the wax seal. Trying to break the wax seal with his fingernail proved futile. Bracing himself on the chest and standing up slowly, he stumbled back to the mesa in his bare feet. Selecting the small metal blade, he worked his way slowly around the box, cutting through the wax. Pulling on the lid, he cracked open the box and looked inside. There he saw an oily white cloth. Unraveling the cloth, he found it contained strips of carne seco, dried meat. His heart rose, and then sank. *Mierda, I can't chew this.*

Looking around, his eyes focused on the small metal bowl, and the solution came to him. He tore the carne seco into small pieces and placed them into the bowl. Covering the meat with water, he placed the bowl on top of the lamp. While the concoction heated, he sat back down and slipped into his new sandals. Soon, the meat softened, and he was able to fill his starving belly with the delicious stew.

Lifting the lamp from the floor, he centered it on top of the mesa. Picking up each of the small bottles he examined their contents using his eyes and his nose. Unable to identify the substances within, he shrugged, returning the bottles to their place. Looking slowly from one object to the next, his eyes stopped on the small leather bound book. Picking it up, he noticed that the cover was decorated with embossed symbols. Tracing the designs with his finger, he attempted to translate their meaning.

The center symbol appeared to be the sun with a spiral inside. Surrounding this symbol were four other symbols, one in each corner. Drifting backward in time, searching through memories of his Brujo Blanco training with his Abuélo, Jesús wondered if these four symbols represented the flowers of sacred plants. One of them, on the top left, looked similar to the flower of the borrachero, or devil's breath. The one on the top right might be the ololiuqui flower, known as the grave plant.

Drifting his fingers downward, Jesús traced one of the lower designs. He whispered the name of the plant, "Huacacachu." The gringos called it Angel's trumpet. The last design on the left was a mystery. Jesús wondered if it represented the flower of the rare hikuli cactus, the one his Abuélo called "hikuli of greatest authority." It was the most powerful of all hallucinogenic cacti. It rendered the user capable of sorcery and deception, but could drive a man mad in the desert if he has not been properly instructed by a skilled Brujo. Jesús believed this was the cactus his Abuélo was asked to identify at the University, so many years ago.

Trembling, Jesús carefully opened the book, hearing the leather creaking and groaning as if in pain. The room was darkening noticeably and Jesús felt the hairs on the back of his neck rising. He closed the book. Spinning around, he searched the room for movement. Only his shadow was moving. Turning his eyes to the lamp, he saw the flame was struggling to stay alive. Gently shaking the lamp with one hand, he realized it was almost out of oil. Admonishing himself, he thought, *Jesus! It's only a book, Jesús.*

Using the sleeve of his robe to protect his hand, he carefully removed the globe from the lamp. Using the remaining flame, he lit one of the candles and extinguished the lamp flame. While it cooled, he found the bottle of oil and refilled the well of the lamp. Turning it over once to wet the wick, he used the candle flame to relight the lamp and replaced

103

the globe. The room brightened considerably. Blowing out the candle, Jesús returned to the book.

Opening the book once again, he squinted at the writing on the first page. Feeling the material between his thumb and forefinger, Jesús knew it was not paper, but some type of skin, pounded, stretched and worked into pages.

The writing was an archaic language, some type of Romance dialect, written by a shaky hand. There were twelve lines on that first page. He was unable to translate the script word for word, but the words *peligroso* or *periculosus*– dangerous, showed up several times.

Jesús noticed his fingers were trembling and a wave of goose bumps washed down his arms and back. At the bottom of the page there was a signature, consisting of several words, yet they were illegible except for the ending name *de Ultrera* and his title: *Brujo Blanco Superior*, suggesting the author was the leader or number one chamanés - sorcerer.

Turning to the next page, Jesús ran his finger slowly down the edge, counting the lines. Once again, there were twelve lines on the page. It appeared to be a directory of the contents of the book. Each line started with the same words, *Yerbos y plantas*. He also found the words *Mortifera , Mortifera desupra, Cura,* and *Evocatio Spiritualis*. Jesús was realizing this was a book of plant recipes and incantations of an ancient master Brujo Blanco. They were recipes for dealing death, death from above, cures, and for summoning spirits. *But these were never to be written down,* he protested. His Abuélo never wrote down any of his teachings and demanded that Jesús commit everything to memory. *This is blasphemy,* he thought angrily.

Feelings of ambivalence were rising through his chest. Part of him wanted to continue reading while another part wanted him to rip the book apart and burn it. Always the curious man, Jesús found himself unable to resist turning the pages. He found later sections entitled *Arca Deus* – meaning Doorway or Entrance to the Stars. and one entitled *Vires, Vita et Vi* – Power, Life and Force. Sitting down on the chest, he began studying and memorizing the entire book.

Chapter 11   Wednesday. Mendoza Reunited

"Ropes" Danzinger – climber, tracker, survival expert, and point man, exited the aircraft first, his blue eyes scanning in all directions. Lucas Forge followed, with tall and skinny Sparks bringing up the rear. All three wore dark sunglasses and had shouldered their carry-on backpacks, freeing their hands so they could silently communicate using hand signals. To the uninitiated, they looked like tourists, casually moving in line with all the other passengers, marching through the metal umbilical accordion tube connecting the aircraft to the gate. Lucas had sent a text to Carlos, notifying him of their arrival at the gate.

Ropes hated being in the gangway's "fatal funnel" that afforded them few options for cover or concealment. He was too short to see above the heads of the passengers in front of him, and had to rely on tall Sparks to observe both the route ahead and the rearward passage.

Sparks stopped suddenly, causing the passenger behind him to bump into him. Looking over his shoulder, he smiled and apologized to the embarrassed woman, but Sparks was surreptitiously scanning the other passengers in line behind him. Turning forward and pretending to only shift the straps on his backpack, he signaled to Lucas.

Male, black jacket, sunglasses, seven back.

Glancing over his shoulder toward Sparks, Lucas nodded. *Got him*. Turning back around he reached out and touched Ropes' left elbow. Looking down, Ropes watched Lucas' hand relay the message, and nodded without looking back.

Exiting into the waiting area, the three looked around in mock confusion. Ropes exclaimed loudly,

"I'm going to the bathroom."

Before he turned around, he shifted his straps as he signaled to the others.

Another one, Male, black T-shirt, bald, sitting, right.

Lucas nodded and stopped. He and Sparks now faced each other pretending to chat while looking at a map of Mendoza produced by Sparks. Lucas spotted the potential threat sitting down, fingering a cell phone. The man looked up and spotted the red-haired Ropes making a quick march straight toward the restrooms. He jumped up and followed Ropes down the corridor.

Out of the corner of his eye, Sparks watched as the man from the plane in the leather jacket emerged from the gangway and moved out of the way to his right. The man looked up at the signs in the waiting area. He began fingering his cell phone nervously.

Ropes bounded into the restroom and quickly made certain it was empty. He slid into the first stall, locking it behind him. He stood on the commode with one foot and launched himself over the divider into the next stall, spinning and landing on the edge of the commode.

The bald man in the T-shirt rushed into the room and slid to a stop. Surveying the room he spotted the locked stall. He moved in front of the stall and lashed out with his right foot, kicking the door open.

Before the man could regain his balance, Ropes pulled his door open, jumped out of his stall and executed a perfect reverse roundhouse kick to the back of the man's neck. The bald man crumpled, his face striking the edge of the commode with a bone crushing crack before slumping unconsciously to the floor.

Ropes methodically searched the man's pockets, retrieving a wallet, some folded papers and the man's cell phone. He lifted the limp body onto the commode and tried to close the door. The lock was hanging uselessly by one bent screw.

"Shit," Ropes mumbled.

Reaching into a side pocket of his backpack he removed a roll of duct tape. Tearing off a piece, he used it to lock the stall. Once again, he jumped over the divider and exited through the open stall.

Sliding over to the sink, he washed his hands. Grabbing a paper towel, he casually exited the restroom, almost bumping into a short fat man who was hurrying inside with a desperate look on his face.

As he turned right down the hallway toward baggage claim, Ropes adjusted his backpack and signaled to his friends.

One down.

Lucas' eyes narrowed slightly. Lucas and Sparks waited for five full minutes before following Ropes down the hallway. Lucas could not suppress his smile after secretly watching the man in the leather jacket trying to act nonchalantly, betrayed by the man's grinding of his teeth and his shifting of his weight from foot to foot.

Checking the signs around the baggage carousels, Ropes found their flight number. A small crowd of people was still gathered around the moving belts, searching for their bags. Moving to the far end of the carousel, Ropes scanned the crowd while waiting for the set of large duffle bags.

He was hoping no one had yet found the unconscious man he left in the bathroom stall.

Lucas and Sparks were moving with the few remaining passengers heading outside to the pickup area. Pushing through the exit doors, Lucas felt the cool humid air slipping across his face. The odor of gasoline and diesel exhaust assaulted his nostrils. Hesitating briefly, he made a quick scan of the sidewalk and roadway, but he concentrated mostly on the people and the vehicles, before exiting fully.

Inside the terminal, nearly the entire crowd had dispersed by the time their duffle bags snaked their way around to where Ropes was waiting. Sliding his sunglasses on top of his hat and reaching out with his abnormally long arms, Ropes snatched the three large bags, swinging them one by one around to his back. An old man wearing a long white beard and an ancient cowboy hat stared at the red-haired Ropes, who now looked like a misshapen pack mule. The old man nudged the short old woman with long gray hair tied into a braid standing next to him. She also started staring at Ropes. Moving toward the exit, Ropes saw their leathered faces and wide eyes. Tilting his head, he asked. "What?"

The old man's face dropped into a frown, while the woman opened her mouth into a flirtatious, but one-toothed smile. Ropes smiled back, thinking *I'll bet she was a real beauty in her time.*

The old man grabbed her elbow and jerked her back around to face the carousel. Keeping his eyes on Ropes as the red-haired Americano and his pile of bags moved passed them, the old man straightened his back and puffed out his chest. The old man's eyes flashed a warning. Ropes lowered his own eyes and waved his free hand in what he hoped communicated an apology. *Geeze, I'll bet that old guy has been through dozens of fights over her.* Slipping his sunglasses back over his eyes, Ropes quickened his pace.

The few remaining people opened a pathway as Ropes plowed his way toward the exit. Muscling his body through the doors, he did a quick scan of the area. Lucas was to his left, leaning against the building and looking at the sparse oncoming traffic. Sparks was seven meters to the right, slowly scanning in both directions. Moving toward Lucas, Ropes lowered the bags, setting them in a neat pile next to the curb. Unzipping one of the bags, he removed his To-Go bag, setting it on top of the other duffle bags. Ropes glanced at the man in the leather jacket who was nervously puffing on a cigarette and standing a meter in front of Sparks.

Sparks signaled to Ropes, who turned and quickly looked at Lucas long enough to see Lucas nod. Reaching down to the pile of bags, Ropes selected his To-Go bag, unzipped a pocket and pulled out a pack of cigarettes.

Lucas heard, shortly before spotting, Carlo's Land Cruiser slowly cruising toward them. Raising his arm, he greeted Carlos with a wave, and a message. Carlos nodded and pulled over in front of Sparks. The few remaining passengers were climbing into cars, pickups and taxis.

Ropes was already moving toward Sparks and the man in the leather jacket. He tapped out a cigarette, holding it between his fingers while slipping the box into his shirt pocket. He made a show of patting his pants and shirt pockets, ostensibly looking for a lost lighter. Lucas heaved the bags over his shoulders and quickly moved to the back of Carlos's truck, opening the rear hatch.

While Lucas secured the bags inside the vehicle, Ropes approached the smoking man and held up his cigarette while asking, "Got a light, amigo?"

The man tensed noticeably, but reflexively reached into his pants for his lighter. Sparks sprang forward and drove a needle into the man's neck. The cigarette fell from the man's mouth as his knees buckled. Sparks grabbed him from the right while Ropes hung on to the falling man from the left. The man's chin dropped to his chest before the cigarette hit the ground. They held him up while moving toward the truck.

Lucas opened the side door of the Land Cruiser and slid across the rear seat. Ropes and Sparks dragged the unconscious man to the open door. Glancing over his shoulders, Ropes spotted the old man and his wife moving through the exit doors, staring at Ropes with wide-eyed confusion.

Ropes and Sparks pushed while Lucas pulled their captive inside Carlo's truck. Sparks climbed inside the back seat next to him and closed the door.

Ropes looked back toward the old couple and shrugged. He offered an explanation to the old man.

"Borrachero. Too much cerveza."

The old man frowned, shaking his head, his eyes still flashing anger toward Ropes. The old women smiled coyly. Shrugging again, Ropes climbed into the shotgun seat as Carlos began driving away.

"Christ, I can't take you anywhere," Carlos announced to his passengers. Ropes guffawed loudly, eliciting smiles from the team as they scanned in all directions.

Carlos adjusted his rear view mirror and locked eyes with Lucas.

"Lucas, what the hell are you wearing?"

Momentarily confused, Lucas looked down at his shirt and pants. He was wearing the light blue shirt and clashing light green cargo pants that looked like all the same color to his color-blind eyes. He looked from one man to the next and pleading ignorance. "What?"

Ropes guffawed even louder, and was joined by loud laugher from Carlos and Sparks.

Carlos shook his head sadly.

"Christ, now I really can't take you anywhere."

Lucas crossed his arms across his chest, looking out the window in mock humiliation.

"Fuck all of you."

Turning back toward Sparks he asked, "Why didn't you say something?"

"Who me?" Sparks shrugged. "I thought you were trying to be, uh, felicitous.

Carlos and Ropes glanced at each other trying to stifle more laughter while pretending to focus on the road in front of them. It didn't work. Ropes snorted and then burst out with another loud guffaw. Sparks and Carlos joined in.

"Ha, ha, ha," Lucas groaned. "OK, new rule. What are we up to, rule 33? New rule. Whenever one of you knuckleheads sees me dressed, uh, felicitously, you are ordered to inform me before we go out in public. Understand?"

The other three men straightened their backs and in unison gave mock salutes toward Lucas. In unison, they responded loudly with "Sir, Yes Sir!"

Under his breath, Lucas spat, "Fuckers. Immature, condescending bastards, all of you."

Breaking the tension, Carlos inquired, "So who's your new friend?"

Sparks responded by searching the man's pockets and checking for weapons. He found a wallet and handed it to Lucas while he began examining the man's cell phone.

Lucas announced, "His license says he is Adelberto Hernandez, 30 years old, and he lives in Mendoza. His address looks like a Ritzy part of town. He has a tattoo on his neck with a weird symbol that I don't recognize."

Carlos glanced back at the man's exposed neck. "I recognize it. I've seen several more just like it in the past 24 hours."

"Trouble?" Lucas asked.

"Nothing I couldn't handle." Carlos reached under his seat, pulling out a plastic bag with four wallets and four cell phones. He handed the bag back to Sparks. Sparks pensively examined the back of Carlos' head for a few moments before he began examining the cell phones' data.

Sparks asked quietly, "Where are they now?"

"Burning in hell, I hope. Except for the kid; I let him go. Word of advice, don't drink the water," Carlos advised.

Sparks and Lucas exchanged a brief look, simultaneously inhaling and exhaling deeply.

Carlos continued, "Frankly, we are wasting our time if we try to get anything out of, uh, Adelberto. At 30 years old, he's been in too long to ever talk to us. He'll die with his secrets. We should just take him to join the others."

Lucas looked out the back window. "Are we being followed?"

Carlos adjusted his rear-view mirror. After several seconds, he answered.

"The man who was going to pick up Adelberto must have, uh, fallen asleep. It will be some time before he awakens."

Ropes studied Carlos' tanned and hardened face. Raising an eyebrow, he nodded to himself.

"You have been a busy little Boy Scout," he noted, with an approving tone.

Carlos stared straight ahead with that thousand yard stare.

They rode in silence for several more minutes. Sparks continued examining the cell phones. He reached into his backpack and pulled out some wires and one of his homemade electronic devices. One by one he connected the phones to his device and fiddled with the icons on the screen.

Finally, Lucas broke the heavy silence. "We should at least give Adelberto a chance to redeem himself."

Carlos continued to stare straight ahead. After a minute, he inhaled deeply and nodded in agreement.

Without looking up from his screen, Sparks offered, "I have something new that might help get him talking."

None of the others bothered to ask him what he meant. Sparks was always experimenting with new electronic devices and new pharmaceutical concoctions. The others had learned not to question him. They could rarely understand his explanations anyway. It sufficed for them to be amazed at his inventiveness, and his results. He held multiple degrees in computer science and neuropharmacology and was a certified EMT, although he never actually went out on emergency calls.

Carlos eventually slowed the Land Cruiser and turned off of the highway on to a dirt road. Lucas kept watch out of the rear window for several kilometers, peering through the large dust cloud kicked up behind them. Carlos drove like a maniac while the three others hung on the best they could. Sparks hung on to the overhead strap with one hand while using his other hand to hold on to his electronics. Their unconscious passenger was thrown around like a rag doll and started moaning.

117

The Land Cruiser went airborne over a large mound in the road as the passengers went weightless for a brief moment of relief, until the wheels hit the dirt and bounced them around once more. No one complained, accepting that Carlos was somehow always in control as he was 'one with his machine'.

After a few more kilometers Carlos pulled up to an abandoned ranch house and maneuvered around to the back, pulling inside of the remnants of an old barn. He switched off the motor. They all sat in silence waiting for the dust to settle as they peered out of the windows into the dim lit barn. Ropes absently made the sign of the cross, thanking God for a safe arrival. A faint smile crossed Carlos' lips.

Without a word, Lucas, Ropes and Carlos exited the hissing and creaking Land Cruiser and efficiently examined their surroundings to ensure they were alone. Carlos opened the rear door of the truck and unzipped a large duffle bag. He selected two Springfield XDM .40 pistols, identical to the one holstered on his right side. He removed an additional XDM 9mm. He handed the .40s to Lucas and Ropes, and gave the 9mm model to Sparks, who was exiting through the passenger door. Once Lucas and Ropes completed their chamber checks and mag. checks, they each holstered their weapons. Sparks carried his 9mm at the ready position while searching the barn.

Carlos found and dragged a couple of ancient sawhorses to the open area in front of his truck.

Ropes found a couple of wide planks and dropped them on top of the sawhorses, forming a makeshift table. Sparks found a rickety bench and sat down with his electronics, continuing his work on the cell-phones. He set his 9mm on the bench next to him.

Lucas kept watch while Ropes and Carlos dragged the moaning passenger out of the vehicle and dropped him on the table. Lucas reached into Carlos' bag and removed a neatly rolled packet of rope. Throwing it to Ropes, he searched the bag until he found the set of four Leatherman multipurpose 'pocket wonder' tools. He set one down next to the 9mm sitting on the bench next to Sparks and handed two others to Ropes and Carlos.

 Sparks ignored this but the other three attached the tools to their belts. Lucas returned to the bag and removed a handful of loaded magazines. He carefully separated the two 9mm mags from the four .40 magazines. He slipped two of the .40 magazines into his mag pouch and set the 9mm magazines next to Spark's 9mm and his pocket wonder.

Walking back to Ropes, he inserted the remaining .40 magazines into Ropes' mag pouch, while Ropes worked on tying the man's hands stretched out above his head. He finished tying up his end seconds before Carlos was finished with the man's ankles. Ropes dramatically raised his hands above his head like a rodeo star, enjoying his win over

Carlos. He did a little victory dance while Carlos rolled his eyes.

The man was waking up now, and started struggling with the bindings, while looking fearfully around the barn and at his captors. A rapid fire string of profanity spurted from his lips. Carlos merely looked down at him until he stopped struggling. Looking menacingly into the man's eyes, Carlos slowly removed his knife from its sheath, holding the point of the blade close to the man's widening eyes.

Somehow, the man found his inner strength and spat at Carlos, who quickly moved aside. The man was obviously impressed with Carlos' speed.

Carlos growled, "I'm in a hurry, pendejo. You have five minutes to tell me who sent you and why you are following us. If you don't, you will leave here blind, deaf, and mute. Your choice."

Sparks stopped moving his fingers, looking over toward Carlos. Standing up, he started to move toward the truck, when Lucas held out a hand to stop him. Sparks looked questioningly into Lucas' eyes. He knew that look. It meant he had forgotten something, once again. He hated when anyone, especially Lucas, caught him in a mistake. He quickly looked at his three teammates and then looked down at his own belt.

"Shit. Sorry, Lucas."

Sparks turned back to the bench and quickly fastened the holster, mag pouch and Leatherman to his belt. He indexed the spare magazines and inserted them into his pouch. Picking up the 9mm, he performed a chamber check and mag check, and holstered his firearm. Turning around, his face was reddening as he waited for Lucas' inspection, but Lucas wasn't there.

Turning his head, Sparks saw Lucas standing next to Ropes. *Shit, shit, shit*, he said to himself, berating himself harder than Lucas ever would.

OK, OK. I can redeem myself, he assured himself. Stepping to the rear of the truck, he found his duffle bag and unzipped it. Pulling apart the opening, he found his large leather clad case, removing it from the bag. Fiddling with the combination locks, he snapped the case open. Looking inside the case, his finger slid across the dozens of vials until he found the one he was looking for. Lifting up the shelf containing the vials, he peered underneath until he found a syringe, a cotton ball, and an alcohol swab packet. Biting down on the plastic needle cover, he removed the cover from the needle and spat out the cover onto the dirt floor.

Inserting the needle into the cap of the vial, he suctioned 10mm of the yellow fluid into the syringe. Holding the needle upwards, he flicked the syringe and pushed on the plunger to expel the bubbles. Walking around the truck, he slowly approached the man on the table. Ropes and Lucas

121

saw him coming and backed away from their captive. Carlos noticed the movement and looked back over his shoulder toward the approaching Sparks, who looked vaguely like a mad scientist. Looking back into the eyes of their captive, Carlos shook his head slowly.

"Time's up, vato."

Carlos held down the man's shoulders while Ropes held his feet. Sparks opened the alcohol swab and rubbed it on the man's neck.

"Sorry. I forgot to do this last time. I hope you don't get an infection." He inserted the needle into the man's carotid and pushed the plunger slowly. Standing up, he took a few steps back and waited.

The man struggled for a few seconds, starting to swear, and then his pupils dilated. His face reddened and his mouth opened wide as he let out a scream. He strained at the ropes binding him to the makeshift table. Carlos covered the man's mouth until the scream stopped and the man became quiet.

Carlos looked back toward Sparks, who nodded slowly. Carlos resumed his interrogation.

"Can you hear me?"

The man slowly nodded.

"Who sent you?"

A few seconds passed in silence. Carlos looked back at Sparks who continued staring at their captive's face.

Slowly, the man started moving his lips, but only a gurgling sound emerged. He looked into Carlos' eyes. Suddenly, he struggled to speak. He wanted to speak to Carlos. He wanted to bare his soul. He wanted to reveal his deepest, darkest, most embarrassing secrets. He wanted to empty his mind of everything he once tried to keep locked away. Finally, the words came.

"Sanchez. Don Benigno Sanchez. El Brujo Superior."

Chapter 12   Wednesday. Mendoza. José and María

Speaking in hushed tones, Lucas consulted with Sparks about the condition of their captive.

"Is your drug going to kill him?"

Sparks feigned his best offended expression.

"Lucas, you know I am not a murderer. No, the drug will not kill him, but it is unlikely that he will remember anything from when we picked him up at the airport. At least for another hour or two, he will not be able to form any new memories. He will only remember following us outside of baggage claim. He might not even remember Ropes asking him for a light. You see, it's a derivative of several cannabinoids and Versed that shut down the hippocampus and…"

"Come on, Sparks," Lucas interrupted. "I don't need to know the details. If what you say is true, we need to get him back to the airport and leave him somewhere. Can he walk?"

Looking at the man still tied to the bench, Sparks thought a few moments.

"I. uh, really don't know. He is, uh, the first test subject."

Lucas was studying Spark's face.

"Jesus, you mean we might have killed him, because you don't know?"

Carlos, leaning against the hood of his truck, was smiling at the intense dialog between his two friends. He interjected, "Why don't I just kill him and we can get on with it. We have a dinner date, and I am getting hungry."

Turning his gaze on to Carlos, Lucas studied him, wondering if he was serious. *What has happened to you? Why are you so thirsty for killing?* Finally he made a decision.

"No. We don't need to kill him, Carlos. If he is not going to remember any of this, we can just dump him. Sparks, can you put some kind of tracker on him?"

Sparks rolled his eyes.

"Do you really have to ask?"

Looking at the dirt floor for a few moments, Lucas raised his head and announced,

"Okay. Untie him and see if he can walk to the truck. Sparks, light him up with one of your devices, but only if you can put it where it won't be found. If he can't walk, we will just sit him on one of the benches outside of baggage claim, and then take off. If he can walk, then we will just help him to the sidewalk and let him wander around. Maybe

he'll get arrested for public intoxication or
something. Maybe he'll walk in front of a bus and
our problem will be solved permanently."

Shaking his head, Carlos silently agreed to the plan,
knowing it was useless to protest.

Ropes didn't care either way and busied himself by
untying the silent captive.

Standing him up, Ropes removed his hands from
the man's shoulders and pointed him toward the
truck. The man stood dumbly, but remained
motionless. After a slight push from Ropes, the man
started walking slowly toward the truck. It appeared
that he was going to continue walking in a straight
line past the truck, so Carlos nudged him toward the
back seat. Surprisingly, he climbed in and sat down.

Lucas frowned at Sparks and ordered him to place
the tracker. From the rear of the truck, Sparks was
searching though his bag until he found the
miniature device. It was about the size and
configuration of a hearing aid battery with a short
wire trailing out of one side. Removing his pocket
wonder, he reached over and made a small set of
incisions on the inside of the man's leather belt. The
man was staring straight ahead and made no move
to protest. Inserting the device inside of the man's
belt, Sparks finished by closing up the incision with
a thin line of super glue.

Returning to his bag, Sparks removed a compact radio receiver and pressed a button to power up the LCD screen. Pressing a few more buttons, he found the small pulsing red dot superimposed on a GPS map of their current location. Turning toward Lucas, he proudly announced,

"It will track his location to within a few meters, as long as he is within a twenty kilometer range of the receiver."

Lucas finally smiled at him and said, "Good job, Sparks!"

Sparks straightened up and shyly returned the smile. *Redeemed at last.*

"Okay, let's roll", Lucas announced.

Arriving at the baggage claim entrances, Carlos steered the truck to the curb. Lucas and Ropes opened the passenger side door, coaxing the man out of the vehicle. Looking around, Lucas spotted only a few people waiting for their rides, all facing in the opposite direction. Ropes gave the man a gentle nudge, and the man started walking slowly toward the exit doors of the baggage claim. They climbed back into the truck and Carlos drove away cautiously.

Lucas turned toward Carlos and asked, "Where are we headed?"

Keeping his eyes on the road, Carlos replied,

"José invited us for dinner. I thought you could use some home cooking."

Lucas beamed, "Maria's asada? This trip keeps getting better."

Carlos continued driving carefully, obeying the local speed limits, fighting his eagerness. Despite their friendship, the team was strangely quiet. Each of the men was lost in their private thoughts, reviewing the day's events. Pulling into the parking lot of José's store, Carlos glanced at his watch. He parked at the far end of the lot, but turned facing the entrance of the store. There were only two other vehicles in the parking lot. The team automatically chose their surveillance quadrants.

"We are a few minutes early. José should be out soon."

Carlos kept the truck running, partly to keep the air conditioner pumping cool air into the cabin. Keeping to his word, José exited the store at 7 pm and locked the doors behind him. He glanced into the reflection of the glass door, spotting Carlos' truck without acknowledging that he saw them. Sliding the accordion steel gate closed, he secured the store, turned, and walked to his pickup.

Climbing behind the wheel, José coaxed the ancient pickup into life. It groaned and sputtered until finally a large blue cloud of smoke bellowed out of the exhaust pipe. Backing out of his space, he drove toward his hacienda, checking his rear-view mirror to ensure that Carlos was behind him.

Twenty minutes later, José turned down an unpaved road. Carlos continued driving down the main road for several kilometers before pulling a U-turn. Satisfied that they were not being followed, he turned into the dirt road, following it to José's home.

José's hacienda was set far back from the dirt road. It was set into the edge of a foothill and the nearest neighbors were several kilometers away. The hacienda was in front, and they could see a half-dozen smaller casitas spread out behind it. Acres of grape vines rolled off into the distance. As they approached the hacienda, the men caught the odor of mesquite and cooked flank steak and onions. Their stomachs began to churn involuntarily and their mouths began to water.

Pulling in behind José's pickup, the men jumped out of the truck eagerly before Carlos stopped. José and Maria were standing on the porch, but Maria rushed out to meet them. Maria planted wet kisses on all of the men in turn. Lucas was last, and he lifted Maria off the ground and spun her around, while she squealed in pleasure. She was very short and had her long gray hair tied back into a braid.

José took his turn and crushed each of the men in a bear hug, eliciting groans of real pain from every one of them.

"Mi casa es su casa," José greeted them in the traditional manner.

Carlos produced a large expensive bottle of Tequila Crema, and presented it to José. His eyes lit up at the precious liquid pleasure.

Oh, Grácias, muchas grácias, mi amigo, but you shouldn't have."

They all laughed heartily at his false protest.

Ushering the men into the dining area, José set the bottle on the tile countertop. Spotting three beautiful women already seated at the far end of table, Carlos hesitated in the doorway. His friends bumped into his back because of his sudden stop. The three women were engaged in some deep female conversation that must have been funny as they were all laughing. A half-empty bottle of tequila, a mound of cut up limes, salt shakers, and several empty shot glasses sat between them. Stopping their laughter suddenly as they saw the men standing awkwardly in the doorway, the women looked them over with smiling faces.

"Señor Cholla!" Antonia cried out, a little too loudly, standing up a little unsteadily. She was radiant in her little black dress and long blond tresses. Her lovely hands were smoothing her very short dress and then reaching up, she slowly brushed her hair back, smiling at Carlos.

The other three men gazed at her in awe and, in unison they turned, looking at Carlos' face. *Son of a gun, he's blushing a little*, Lucas thought.

Carlos was already rushing toward her, reaching out and then gathering her up in his arms, lifting her up, and spinning her around. Tilting her head back, her long blond hair was flowing like a thick cloud. Setting her down, Carlos nestled her face in his hands. Looking deeply into her large blue eyes, he drew her in for a long kiss. She gave him no resistance. Her arms encircled his strong back as her fingers were burrowing into his hair and her knees buckled.

Leaning against the counter, José was smiling broadly at the spectacle in front of him. Maria was also watching from the entrance to her cocina, her hands pressed palm to palm in front of her face, as if she were praying. Her eyes locked with José's, exchanging knowing smiles.

With widening eyes, the other two women were also looking at each other exchanging some mysterious communication.

Clearing his throat, and standing erect, José cut the sexual tension. "I hope you do not mind, but we have some dinner guests. Our niece invited her friend to visit Argentina and explore the vineyards of Mendoza. They are staying with us for a week before moving on to Buenos Aires."

Looking at the men standing in the doorway, José announced, "Allow me to present my sobrina, my niece, Señorita Marianna Montoya.

Tearing their eyes away from the tempestuous tango that was Carlos and Antonia, Lucas and the others entered the room, giving full attention to the young woman who was standing up slowly and carefully from the table. All three men turned their gaping mouths into their best brilliant smiles.

Marianna was unlike the petite blond Antonia in almost every way. She had her auburn hair tied up in a loose bun, with wisps of hair floating around her face and head. Her flawless skin was the color of golden oak and her large flashing eyes contained dark, almost black irises. Her hunter green silky dress broke an inch above her knees, revealing shapely calves accentuated by her high heeled matching shoes. The dress was straining to contain her voluptuous curves, topped off by a modest neckline and short sleeves.

Elbowing Lucas out of the way, Ropes hurried forward, extending his hand. Flashing a return smile, Marianna took his hand and gracefully curtsied. Ropes was stunned into staring a little too long at her hypnotic eyes before catching himself and stammering out a greeting.

"Wow, I mean, I, uh, I am very pleased to meet you, Marianna. My name is uh Richard, but my uh friends call me Ropes."

"Hello, 'uh Richard'," she teased, speaking in melodic accented English. "I am very pleased to encounter you as well."

Standing like statues and locking eyes for several more seconds, their greeting was finally interrupted by Lucas, who was now standing next to Ropes with his hand out.

"Encantado, Señorita Montoya, I am Lucas, Lucas Forge."

Turning to face him, Marianna's smile faded ever so slightly as she tilted her head slightly and then, pulling her hand free from Ropes' grip, she took Lucas' hand, but did not curtsy.

"I am pleased to meet you again, Señor Forge. We actually met many years ago when I was just a little girl maybe 10 years of age. My uncle has told me many amusing stories of you and your adventures."

Looking at José with confusion on his face, he suddenly realized this was "little" Marianna all grown up. José laughed at his confusion and explained,

"I told you Lucas, fresh mountain air, fresh vegetables, and Maria's asada combine to work miracles."

"I can see that now, amigo," Lucas nodded, appreciating Marianna's beautiful transformation.

Clearing his throat nervously, Sparks suddenly appeared next to Lucas, taking his turn at elbowing Ropes out of the way.

Bowing formally, he greeted her by taking her hand and saying, "Buenas noches, Señorita Montoya. I am Sheldon Sparks, but everybody calls me Sparks. I am happy to meet you."

Marianna curtsied and returned the greeting. "Buenos noches, Sparks."

Turning back toward the table, Marianna reached out with her left arm toward the third woman, who was still seated at the table.

"May I present to you my dearest friend and distant cousin, Stephania Alvarez."

Placing her hands on the table for balance, Stephania stood up and carefully moved around the table to stand next to Marianna.

She was taller than she appeared when sitting down behind the table, and was quite slender, almost skinny, especially standing next to the much shorter and curvy Marianna. Her long black hair was pulled tightly against her head by an intricate braid ending at her waist. Her dark gray dress stopped an inch above her knees, highlighting her long slender legs. Her short jacket was a multicolor cacophony of various silk patterns, contrasting with her almost bookish hairstyle and black rimmed glasses accenting her light brown eyes.

Sparks was smitten. All eyes were on the two tall skinny forms as Sparks reached out and clasped her delicate hand in both of his own.

Bowing formally and mimicking Lucas' words, Sparks spoke slowly and softly, "Encantado, senorita Alvarez. I am delighted to make your acquaintance."

Laughing at his formality, Stephania replied in English with a slight British accent, "Good evening, señor 'everyone calls me Sparks.' Everyone calls me Steffi."

Straightening from his bow, Sparks smiled shyly, repeating her name, "Steffi. That's nice. I like it."

It was his turn to be nudged away by Ropes. Releasing her hand and moving to her side, he watched her closely as she moved gracefully, like a leopard, to greet the other two men.

Breaking away from embracing Antonia, Carlos pulled her toward the group. Sparks never heard their greetings and introductions as he was lost in his own thoughts, repeating her name to himself over and over. *Steffi. Steffi.*

"Sparks?"

"Sparks!" Carlos was almost shouting.

Shaking himself from his reverie, Sparks began focusing on Carlos' face. "What?"

Smiling at Sparks' confusion, Carlos introduced him to Antonia.

"Sparks, may I introduce my, uh, good friend, Señorita Antonia Cabrera."

All three women tensed and looked disappointingly at Carlos' face. He never saw it coming.

Lucas saw it, and understood Carlos' mistake. *That's strange. Carlos usually doesn't screw up when it comes to women.*

Breaking the tension, Sparks reached out his hand to Antonia, bowing once again.

"Señorita Cabrera, I am delighted to finally meet one of Carlos' uh, friends." *That'll teach him*, Sparks thought, smiling at Antonia.

THE MENDOZA CONNECTION

Smiling briefly at Sparks, she took his hand.
Looking over at Carlos, Antonia replied icily, "My
friends call me Antonia."

Oh shit, Carlos thought, finally realizing his grave
mistake. Looking into Antonia's icy blue eyes, he
was at a loss. In desperation, he tried to pull her
closer, giving her his best winning smile. Stiffening,
she resisted, but only for a moment.

Punching him in the arm, not entirely playfully, she
growled, "Friend? FRIEND?"

Seeing that Carlos was in deep trouble, Lucas
pulled out an expensive bottle of Tequila from
under his jacket. Holding it over his head, he loudly
asked, "Tequila shots anyone?"

Everyone turned toward Lucas and cheered.
"Tequila!"

Lucas uncorked the bottle and began pouring shots
all around. "Salt up everyone!" Lucas shouted.
Holding up his own glass when they were ready, he
proposed a toast to their hosts.

"We arrived as strangers to this beautiful land and
found even more beautiful women. Now, thanks to
our equally beautiful hosts, we are no longer
strangers, but, with my apologies to Antonia, we are
now all good… uh friends."

Everyone except Carlos burst into laughter and then licked the salt off of the backs of their hands and swallowed their shots in one gulp, following it with a slice of lime. More laughter ensued.

Lucas smiled at everyone as they all began talking at once. Surveying the room, he suddenly realized that he was the only man without a woman to talk to. Staring at the floor, he began reminiscing.

Maria looked at José from across the room. He smiled and nodded. Maria turned, walking into her cocina. José followed her and they disappeared for a few minutes. They returned with another woman. Shouting to be heard above the laughter, José gently pulled the woman forward to stand in front of him.

"Señors y señoritas! I am pleased to introduce you to our good friend, Alícia Jameson."

Lucas slowly turned to face them, his stomach suddenly flip flopping. Carlos was struck dumb. Staring first at Lucas, then at Alícia, and then back to Lucas, Carlos thought, *Alícia. I looked everywhere for her. Everywhere. How did José find her?*

Oblivious to everyone else, Alícia gazed hesitatingly at Lucas.

"Hello, Lucas," she said simply.

All he could say was "Alícia."

Drinking her in with his eyes, she was exactly as he remembered, except her wavy black hair was a little shorter and she looked a lot thinner, almost fragile. She wore a simple and modest white dress with a high lace collar and long sleeves, with more lace at her wrists. Her dark olive skin contrasted beautifully against the white dress. Her ankles peeked out from the bottom of her dress, and she was held up by gold open toed wedge sandals. Her light green eyes were starting to mist as her hands trembled.

Moving forward, Lucas reached out to her.

"Oh, Lucas," she cried out, closing the last few steps to meet him. Pausing to look into her eyes, he slowly gathered her into his arms. Tears were now flowing freely down her face and began soaking into his jacket. "Oh, Lucas," she whispered.

Everyone was quietly staring at them in curiosity. Grabbing the bottle off of the table, José raised it over his head and shouted, "Mas Tequila anyone?"

The mood shifted instantly as the men shouted back, "Uno Mas!" and the salt shakers were passed around. Even Maria, who rarely drank, joined in.

Holding her by her shoulders, Lucas pulled back so he could see her eyes. Whispering, he asked, "What happened to you? We looked everywhere, but you just disappeared."

Looking down, Alícia whispered back, "It is a long story and a short story; but I am here now, thanks to José." Looking back into his eyes, she pleaded, "Can we talk about it later, please, Lucas. It has been so long since I have been among friends, and I really want to have some fun tonight."

Frowning at first, Lucas could not worry for long. "Of course, my love. Whenever you are ready is fine with me. God, I've missed you."

Alícia smiled at him for the first time in many years. She stepped back and looked him up and down. Her face contorted as she asked a little too loudly, "My God, Lucas, what are you wearing?"

Lucas looked down at his outfit that he thought was very nice. He was still wearing the light blue shirt and clashing light green cargo pants. He topped it off with salmon colored blazer. "What?" was his only answer.

Everyone burst into laughter as his face reddened. Alícia stated the obvious, "Lucas, you really need me to dress you."

Holding her tightly by the hand, as if he was afraid he might lose her again, Lucas grabbed the bottle off of the table. Raising it up over his head, he shouted, "Mas Tequila anyone?"

This time, everyone shouted back, "Uno Mas!" The party was on.

Lucas marveled at Maria's simple, yet elegant presentation on the large wooden table. She created a beautiful centerpiece out of fresh-cut yellow roses and purple lilies. There were tall candles everywhere, making everyone's skin and eyes look radiant. Ten china settings were symmetrically placed around the table. Bowls of fresh salsa in several varieties were generously squeezed in all around. Three large wooden bowls were overflowing with blue corn tortilla chips. Large bowls of fresh salad and vegetables were placed at both ends of the table. José had produced two new bottles of tequila and set them in the middle of the table.

Maria had to shout over the loud conversations, "Please, everyone sit down. La cena is ready." Pulling the chairs out for the women, the men invited them to be seated. Smiling and raising their eyebrows at each other, the four women selected their seats, each next to their chosen companions for the evening. Lucas held the chair for Maria at one end of the table, and she kissed him on the cheek before sitting down.

Walking in from the cocina, José was carrying a huge platter with several bowls of steaming carne asada, fresh hot tortillas, grilled green onions and hot peppers, red radishes, cilantro, and bowls of mashed avocado.

Setting the platter on the counter and lifting his arms, he bowed his head and offered up a heartfelt prayer of gratitude to their God. When he was finished, everyone said, "Amen." He began passing the food around to the eager guests. Bowls started flying around the table, left and right and back and forth, rarely touching the table until everyone started eating and the room grew quieter. The only sounds were exclamations of pleasure and the frequent praises for Maria and José. Maria looked across the table at José as tears of joy ran down her cheeks. José was dabbing his eyes with his napkin and noticed Lucas looking at him.

José grunted, "I got some salsa in my eyes."

Raising his glass, Lucas smiled and replied, "Well then, amigo, here is to salsa tears."

When the eating slowed, Maria lifted a bowl of asada and innocently asked, "Would anyone like some more?"

They all looked at her, and in unison shouted, "Uno mas!"

Standing up from the table, Lucas walked over to the counter and opened the bottle of Tequila Crema. Rounding the table he poured each guest a shot.

"This is for sipping, my friends."

Taking a sip and letting it sit in her mouth before swallowing, Alícia announced excitedly, "This is like dessert!"

Standing up and moving quietly into the cocina, Maria disappeared while José stood up and began clearing the table. The women started to get up to help, but the men told them to stay seated as they began helping José. In minutes, the table was cleared. Maria entered carrying a tray with 10 small bowls of homemade vanilla bean ice cream and containers of hot dark chocolate and hot caramel.

The guests protested weakly, but soon the bowls were empty. Ropes announced, "I can't move anymore." Groans of agreement were uttered by all.

José whispered something in Lucas' ear, and he nodded. Standing up, José announced, "Gentlemen, please join me on the patio for some brandy and cigars. Ladies, you are welcome to join Maria on the front porch. I apologize, but we men have some business to attend to for a short while."

Antonia, Marianna, and Steffi shared hungry wolf-like glances. They were dying to get the scoop on Alícia, who was looking like a deer in headlights. They also wanted to talk about the men on the patio. They all stood up, hanging on the backs of chairs to steady themselves. Grabbing a half-empty bottle of tequila, Antonia raised the bottle, waving it over her head and whispered to the other women, "Mas tequila, anyone?"

Grinning conspiratorially, the three women whispered back, "Uno mas!" Taking Maria's arm, Antonia wobbled toward the porch. Marianna and Steffi held on to each other for support and followed them outside.

José's hacienda was built around an inner uncovered patio. It was filled with potted citrus, avocado, mango, and papaya trees. There was a fire pit in the middle with a crackling fire already burning furiously. Surrounding the pit, were a dozen chairs and folded umbrellas. Each of the men fell into the chairs and began staring into the flames.

José started speaking first, looking around to ensure they were alone.

"Carlos, I have obtained the supplies you requested and reserved the mules at Puente del Inca. Pablo Silva will meet you there at 11:00 am. I know you wanted to get there earlier, but I also knew that tonight would be filled with tequila and, uh dessert." He smiled knowingly at the last word.

Lucas asked, "Where did you find Alícia?"

Lowering his eyes, José answered, "I think, perhaps, that it is best that she tell you the story herself."

Lucas thought, *That is odd. Why did he look down before answering? What is he hiding? I need to get him alone.*

Turning toward Carlos, he asked, "What is it that you have found that was so important to bring us down here?" He added, "Not that I am complaining."

Reaching inside his leather jacket, Carlos pulled out two pieces of old paper. Smoothing them out on the table next to the fire pit, he fit the ragged edges together.

Standing up, the four men looked down at the papers. José remained behind at a respectful distance, tending to the fire. Carlos spoke, "Look, I found the first piece on the right in the library in Barioloche. I was doing some research on the Brujos. Hidden in one of the ancient books on the Brujos, I found this piece of paper. Someone left it there, but I do not know who.

The second piece on the left I lifted from a mafia goon called El Lion. He said he took orders from Don Benigno. That one appears to be a map of an ancient trail that leads south from Puente del Inca up to the base of Tupungatito volcano. It was torn at the edge before the trail ended. I think Benigno and the mafia goons were using it to somehow protect the trail, or use it for some other reason."

Pointing toward the second piece, he stated, "This one, the one I found in the library, seems to be the continuation of the trail that goes around the back of the Tupungatito volcano and stops at these symbols." The three men were looking closely

145

where Carlos pointed. "I do not know what they mean, but I believe they have something to do with their drug smuggling. Maybe it is an airstrip, or maybe there is a secret road that leads north through the Andes. I can't make heads or tails of it."

Straightening up, Lucas whispered to the others. "You did well, Carlos. This may be what we needed to drive a stake into their smuggling operation." Picking up the paper on the right, he held it out to José, who was pretending to tend to the fire.

"José, do you recognize any of these symbols?"

The old man studied the paper, squinting at the mysterious designs.

"I am not sure, but I think they may represent some types of special plants. My grandfather had a book with symbols like this on the cover. He was a healer of sorts, and I suspected he was an herbalist, or maybe even a Brujo. He never let me touch it, but when he was away, I often looked at it. I did not understand the symbols or the writing, and became bored with it. I do not know what became of it after he died. I am sorry, I cannot help you more."

José continued, "I have six separate casitas on the property, and Maria has made up the beds. My niece and her friend are staying in the second casita. Alícia is in the first casita. You are welcome to take any of the others and make them your homes tonight. There is firewood in each one, in case you wish to build fires. The supplies you wanted are stored inside the first casita. I always awaken before the sun and the damn rooster, so I will have coffee made in the cocina. The leftovers from tonight, meager though they may be, will be in the ice box. Please help yourselves. Is there anything else you need?"

Carlos looked at Lucas through tequila glazed eyes. Trying to make his mind focus, Lucas thought a few moments before replying, "I really can't think of anything else tonight."

Ropes and Sparks were looking at each other, and Ropes signaled to him, *Let's get out of here and find the women.*

Staring at Ropes, Lucas said, "I saw that." Ropes and Sparks returned his stare, and Sparks said, in his best imitation of Lucas, "What?"

They all laughed, standing up and tearing themselves away from the fire. Lucas, turning toward José, said, "My friend, I cannot thank you enough." Reaching into his breast pocket and removing a thick envelope, he handed it to José.

Feeling the weight of the envelope, José protested. "Amigo, no es necessario."

Becoming serious, Lucas looked into his eyes. "José, we do not know when, or if we will return. If we do not, then I have one more favor to ask of you.

147

It is a big one. Please take care of yourself and Maria. If there is any left over, please help Alícia, if she needs it."

Staring into Lucas' eyes, and grasping his hand, José nodded. "I will do as you ask, my friend. Now I must say goodnight as my Maria needs me."

Drawing him in, Lucas gave him a hug. "Thank you, José. No more will be said of this night."

"Vaya con Dios, my friends, vaya con Dios."

Lining up behind Lucas, the other three men hugged José, one at a time, and bid him a good night.

Following José back into the hacienda, they watched as he veered off to his sleeping quarters. The men found their way to the front porch. Maria was gone, but the four women were whispering and giggling among themselves. Lucas reached out to Alícia, and said to the others, "Please excuse us, but we have a lot of catching up to do. It was very nice to meet all of you."

Without saying another word he took her by the hand, leading her to the first casita. He was not concerned with the sleeping arrangements of his friends. It was none of his business.

****

Several hours later, José suddenly awakened from a deep sleep and sat up. He felt something was wrong. Looking at his alarm clock, he saw it was only a little after three o'clock in the morning. Turning over, Maria saw that he was sitting on the edge of the bed. "What is it, José?"

"I do not know. I felt something, uh, I don't know. It felt like something changed; something shifted. I cannot explain the feeling, it just feels wrong somehow."

Reaching out and rubbing his back, Maria said sleepily, "Come lie down, José. I do not feel anything. Try to go back to sleep."

Running his fingers through his hair, he nodded, and taking her advice, he laid back on the bed. Staring up at the ceiling, it was an hour before he slept.

Chapter 13   Wednesday Night.   Mendoza.
Alícia's Tale

Sitting next to each other on the edge of the bed, and turning toward her, Lucas held on to Alícia's hands. She was staring into the fire, so he waited patiently, knowing not to push her until she was ready. Taking a deep breath, she began to speak softly.

"A few months after we were last together here in Mendoza, my father came to me with one of his discoveries. He had been exploring the volcano Tupungatito and found some ancient artifacts. He said that some of them were many hundreds of years old. But he also found pieces of an aircraft in the same place."

"Isn't he always finding artifacts? I mean, that's his job. Why did he come to you?"

Inhaling deeply, she continued.

"Yes, that is his job, but he said these were different. He said they shouldn't be here."

"What did he mean? The artifacts, or the airplane pieces?"

"He said that some of the artifacts were not from the Andes. They were not from the ancient indigenous peoples who once lived here. He thought they resembled the ceremonial artifacts that he once

150

examined when he was working in northern Mexico. He also did not know why there were pieces from some aircraft. He thought that they may be from a British airplane"

"Mexico, British? How did they get down here to Argentina?"

"That just it, Lucas. It did not make any sense to him. So I told him we should show them to José and Maria since they grew up in Mexico and they could trace their origins back centuries to indigenous peoples in central Mexico. You told me once that José knew a lot of the old ones, the people who still performed the old healing ceremonies."

"Well, yes, but that was when he and Maria were very young. They later travelled all over the world together. He fought in many wars as a mercenary and somehow earned a couple of degrees along the way. They finally settled down here in Mendoza almost thirty years ago. I know his memory is phenomenal, but I don't know that he could be much help."

Looking into Lucas eyes, Alícia started trembling. Putting his arm around her, Lucas kissed the top of her head. He wanted to know the whole story right now, but forced himself to let her go at her own pace. After many moments of silence, she continued.

"I brought my father here and he showed the artifacts to José and Maria. It was Maria who provided the most help. It turns out that while José had sat around many fires talking to the old ones and listening to their stories, Maria spent her time talking to the old women. The women were the ones who collected, preserved, and passed on to younger generations most of the old ceremonial artifacts."

Nodding, Lucas said, "I always thought she was the smarter one. Without her, José would have probably ended up dead because of his curiosity. He sometimes asked too many questions of the wrong people." *He seems to have mellowed considerably.*

Alícia continued, "She told my father that he was correct. The artifacts were ceremonial and utilitarian objects used in healing ceremonies. One of them, however, was used by Brujos for some secret purposes. She thought it had something to do with some kind of warfare or battles with other Brujos."

Staring into the fire, Lucas began to focus his powerful mind to sort through the information he had been gathering over the past several years. *Warfare. Brujos. Artifacts. Mexico. Mendoza. Drugs. Murder. Money. Power. Good. Evil. Don Benigno. Drug running. Borders. America. Symbols. Maps.* His head started hurting from the tequila that was interfering with his abilities to make connections among disparate data. He realized that Alícia was staring to talk again.

"Neither José nor Maria could explain why the artifacts were anywhere near a volcano in the Andes. Why were airplane parts mixed in with ancient pottery? It didn't make any sense. Finally my father thanked them for their help and we drove back to my apartment in the city. Before we even got to the outskirts, we were suddenly surrounded by three trucks. They forced us off the road, and many men came out of the trucks pointing guns at us." Alícia began to sob and she gripped Lucas' hand tightly.

Feeling a mixture of concern, fear and anger, Lucas wanted this to all go away. He didn't want her to hurt anymore. He felt guilty that he had not been there to protect her. He wanted revenge on the men who had threatened her. He wanted...but she continued.

"They tied us up and took the artifacts. Then they drove us north for almost two days. They would not speak to us. I thought they were going to kill us, but I found out that they also took care of us. They fed us and gave us clean clothes. Eventually they took us up into the mountains to some type of compound where they imprisoned us. They separated me from my father. They questioned me about the artifacts for days or weeks. I lost track of time. Eventually they stopped questioning me, and I begged them to let me see my father. They never did, and I never saw him again."

Alícia sobbed loudly, her tears running down Lucas shirt. "I don't even know if he is still alive."

Forcing himself to keep quiet, Lucas held her tightly. After a few minutes the sobbing slowed and she became quiet. Taking a few deep breaths, she started again.

"The men kept rotating, new ones arriving, and the ones I knew disappeared. Soon they put me to work in the fields. They had a large vineyard and gardens with many types of plants and cacti. They treated me well, but rarely spoke to me. After many months, I started to work in the kitchen. I could not leave because I did not know where we were and there were no other houses or farms in sight.

Someone was always watching me. One of the men tried to force himself on me and I started screaming. Several other men came running and they killed him right in front of me."

Lucas' anger and guilt was retuning, but he kept silent. Staring into the fire, he imagined what he was going to do to the men if he ever found them.

Alícia continued, "I tried to keep track of the days and months. The seasons changed many times. Every month, four or five large black SUVs arrived and many men in suits and rifles got out. One of the men seemed to be in charge. He was huge and muscular with very long black hair. His skin was dark. I only got close to him once. As he walked by me, he looked into my eyes. I have never felt such pure evil. His eyes were the strangest color gray, almost like pearls. I almost fainted, but he turned away."

Alícia was quiet for a few moments, staring into the dying fire. Feeling drained but relieved to be finally telling someone, anyone, but especially Lucas, the story of her trials, she sighed and squeezed his hand.

"I do not know how long I had been there, but one day, while I was bringing in some water, I saw a single pickup truck coming up the road. Several of the men nearby were talking to each other, and one was talking into a radio or satellite phone. The truck stopped at the gate and one of the guards spoke to the driver for many minutes. They seemed to be arguing until the guard pulled out a radio and listened. The man with the satellite phone came over to me and told me to follow him. We walked all the way to the gate and then he turned and just walked away. The guard waved me over impatiently. I was so beaten down and hopeless, I almost welcomed what I thought was certain death. Then the door to the pickup opened, and the driver got out."

Alícia turned to look Lucas in his eyes. "Lucas, it was José!"

"José?" was all Lucas could say.

"I ran to him and hugged him and cried. I was frantic because I thought we were both going to be killed. But José said a few more words to the guard, and handed something to him, and we both got into the pickup, and he drove me all the way to his hacienda. I have been here only one day."

"I kept asking him to tell me how he found me, but he would not say. The only thing he told me was that he owed you, and that he was overjoyed to find me and that was all I needed to know."

The fire was now a bed of coals with only an occasional flame escaping from its impending death. It was as if the fire knew the story had come to a close.

Lucas was facing the fire, but his eyes were burning with thoughts of revenge. They sat on the bed, quietly lost in their own thoughts for many minutes.

Breaking the silence, Alícia spoke softly, "Lucas, I am very tired. Can we go to sleep now? I just need you to hold me until I fall asleep."

Kissing her gently, Lucas nodded and replied, "Of course, my love. I can't think of anything I want more."

Chapter 14   Thursday night. Benigno Sanchez, Brujo Negro Superior

Franco Fernández forced himself to stop and rest. He had been hiking all day. Now it was night. For the last four hours he had been pushing himself hard, too hard. Sweating from the exertion, and from the stimulant effects of the coca leaves in his mouth, he was feeling internally hot and externally chilled from his sweat drenched robe. His heart was pounding and his lungs were burning. Sitting on a boulder he stared up the trail toward the Tupungatito volcano. He was getting close, but still found no sign of Benigno or most importantly, Luciana.

Something was changing in him, something that been incubating in his mind during the last year. Benigno had been bringing him, and Luciana, into his inner circle. Benigno finally let them in on his megalomaniacal plans. They had accompanied him and his elite cadre of assassins to the northern countries, Brazil, Ecuador, Peru, and the Central Americas. One by one, Benigno's money and influence overpowered their underground criminal and drug distribution networks.

Franco learned Benigno's masterful methods of infiltration and assimilation. They would start with the lowest levels of street criminals and drug pushers, turning them into pawns and informants, dependent upon and loyal to Benigno's cause. Don Benigno then identified those individuals with hidden potential and undervalued talents and offered them Brujo Negro training and advancement. Those who complied would be richly rewarded with money, power and influence. Those who did not comply would be eliminated. In turn, the survivors would move up the chain of command.

With surprising speed, the lieutenants and captains of the underworld organizations would either join him or disappear. Sometimes the coups would be relatively bloodless, but in a few cases the leaders would foolishly resist, ensuring their demise. Benigno would then insert one of his top Brujo Negro disciples to preside over all operations within the countries. A large percentage of the profits always flowed back into Benigno's coffers, funding the next takeovers.

The following stage was often more difficult. Benigno and his disciples would focus on infiltration and assimilation into the governments and especially the media. Again, sometimes the coups would be relatively bloodless. Key officials in the government and in the newspaper and broadcast media were identified. Some would join willingly; others had to be bribed or blackmailed into compliance until the time was right for their elimination and replacement. Common enemies, real or invented, such as multinational corporations, were identified. Political elections were either rigged or won by manipulating the common voters with promises of security, fairness, and prosperity without effort.

Franco and the other twelve disciples were supposedly now at the pinnacle of their training. They came from all over the world, citizens of European countries, Australia, Indonesia, Africa and India. They were the best and the brightest, and Franco resented the indignity of this final initiation.

Benigno promised them secret new powers through something he called The Ascension. He insisted they had to drag themselves into this godforsaken wilderness dressing in these ridiculous robes and sleeping under the stars. He had become used to the finer things in life, fast cars, expensive clothing, and rare wine.

Franco had his own plans. The Benigno he once revered and adored had changed during the past few years. Franco, now almost thirty, no longer craved the father figure he once needed. He noticed that Benigno had become increasingly paranoid, and he was also distracted by certain supernatural tales. His occasional rants drifted into monologues about alien visitors and alien technologies. During one of these recent rants, Franco thought he saw Luciana rolling her eyes.

Benigno taught him well, perhaps too well. Ruthless ambition sometimes required ruthless methods. Almost six months ago, Franco was sent on a solo mission to hunt down and kill one of the few remaining powerful Brujo Negro masters, ensconced in the highlands of the Patagonias. Franco found him and almost lost his life in the ensuing battle.

The master was truly evil and displayed powers that Franco had never seen before. Fortunately, the Brujo was very old and was unable to sustain his attacks for very long. Franco was able to overpower him, partly with the aid of his pistol, but he did not kill the master right away. Instead, supposedly in exchange for the man's life, Franco manipulated him into revealing his secret power spells and a couple of potions that were new to Franco. Once he was drained of his knowledge, Franco drained him of his life.

Franco now possessed powers and knowledge unknown to Benigno. He shared these secrets with no one, not even Luciana. He had begun to practice one of the techniques, the *influencia oculto,* on a few of the thirteen disciples. It was like a posthypnotic suggestion that he could implant into their minds. Later, using a word or hand movement, he could unleash certain mind sets and behaviors in his victims. It was even possible to create a contagious mass effect on others in the vicinity. One victim could affect two, and two could affect four, and soon a whole crowd of people could be influenced. It was similar to mass hysteria or the actions of a mob of people.

He had been waiting for the right opportunity. He needed to find the right moment when Benigno was vulnerable and unprotected. He had not, however, foreseen Benigno's brutal attack on him last night. That was the final straw for Franco. Benigno had humiliated him in front of Luciana, and now Benigno must pay the price.

The moon had disappeared behind the Andes but the stars in the clear sky and thinning air provided plenty of light for his mission. His pupils were dilated from the coca, bringing in more light to his retinas. To Franco, it was almost like daylight under a cloudy sky.

Sniffing the air, he tried to catch her scent. Closing his eyes and concentrating, he inhaled deeply through his nose. He was far above the last of the mountain vegetation, as he had been running among only inorganic rocks and boulders for hours. There were few distracting odors to sort out this time, but one odor dominated his olfactory sense, blocking out everything else; it was the aloe.

Reaching up, he untied the ribbon holding the aloe against his burnt flesh. Peeling the now dried aloe leaves away from his skin, he threw them as far away as he could. Gently folding the stained ribbon, he stuffed it into the side pocket of his pack. Using the toe of his sandal he dug a small hole in the rocky soil beneath his feet. Leaning over, he spat out what was left of the wet coca leaves into the hole. Covering up the hole with the excavated soil, he stood on the small mound, tamping it flat.

Waiting for the odors to disperse into the thin air, he again meditated on the chant against pain, the *Cantar Doler.* The combination of the chant and the coca still in his system forced his pain to diffuse into his footprints. Drinking from his almost empty canteen, he swished the cold water inside his mouth and swallowed to cleanse his palate. Closing his eyes and inhaling deeply, he concentrated once more, searching for her unique scent. He found nothing.

Panicking, he opened his eyes, straining into the distance. Turning his head slightly to the left, and then to the right, he tried using his peripheral vision to catch any sign of them. *Where are they? Where is Luciana?* Reaching into his pack, his fingers searched for more coca. Finding the small handful of leaves left, he pulled out a few of them, stuffing them into his mouth and began chewing furiously.

Waiting for the coca to take effect, he removed a small leather pouch from his pack. Untying the rawhide cord at the top, he shook a dozen coffee beans into his palm. Popping them into his mouth, he began crunching them, mixing the bitter beans with the coca. Sealing the pouch, he returned it to his pack. Removing a small canister containing one of the healing salves he stole from the old Brujo in Patagonia, he rubbed the sticky substance into his wounds and stood up. Hyperventilating to infuse his blood with oxygen, he commanded his body, *Move. Now.*

Starting at a slow trot, he began picking up speed, his legs pumping up the steep trail like a locomotive. Nothing would stop him from finding Luciana, and Benigno.

******

Far ahead, Benigno slowed his pace as he began approaching the summit of the volcano. The imperceptible trail eased into a wide flat shelf. He had been here once before with his mentor, Elisandro, during his final initiation into the Brujo Negros. He remembered thinking that he was going to die on this mountain. Elisandro had forced him up the trail without any water, and when they reached this spot, Benigno had been delirious with thirst. The effects of the coca could no longer override his body's screaming for water. Elisandro had forced Benigno to sit and calm himself, to slow his heart, and to conquer his pain. Together, they had chanted the *Cantar Doler*, until Benigno could focus his mind and senses.

Benigno hated and feared his mentor at that moment, and he had considered trying to smash Elisandro's brains in with a rock and steal his canteen. Elisandro knew this, for he too had been taken to this spot as a young man for his own initiation. He too thought he was going to die on the mountain, and he too thought about killing his

163

mentor for his water. Instead, he learned to control his powerful survival drive for water that would normally force him to do anything to live.

He learned to control his anger and his lust for violence. Elisandro taught him to monitor his emotions, to become aware of when he felt frustration, to search his thoughts to identify what he really wanted and why. Frustration was a powerful motivating force that could help him overcome obstacles, but only obstacles that could be overcome.

Benigno learned that, at times, his obstacles were not worth his energy and resources. It was within his power to decide to keep fighting for solutions or to accept the reality that some things were unchangeable. Frustration could fuel clear thinking, but anger would only unleash the blood lust. Anger would cloud his judgment and drive him toward stupid reactions and unthinking violence.

Benigno was transformed that day on the edge of the mountain. He was transformed from a boy who was ruled by his emotions to a man who could choose his reactions. His realized that his emotions were like a horse that only reacted to the physical world, but he could become like the horse's rider who could control the horse, control the urges and reactions of the horse. He became free and powerful. He became a Brujo Negro master.

Now, many years later, Benigno was the mentor. He had advanced far beyond the powers of Elisandro. He devoted many years to perfecting his understanding of the pharmaceutical properties of the potions and elixirs of the crude pharmacopeia used by Elisandro and the elders of the Brujo Negro. He experimented with new plant extracts and mixtures, testing them on ignorant peasants and homeless beggars. He tested some of them on his enemies. He integrated the ancient Brujo herbalist methodologies with the power of the new sciences, with their microscopes, their mass spectrometry and quantum physics.

Benigno worked in the shadows of a shadowy world and became the hidden godfather of a massive criminal drug cartel. He and his chemists developed new and powerfully addicting drugs that led to the pacification of millions in El Norte, America, who became slaves to his potions. He was able to amass a fortune that provided him with untold luxuries, politicians, officials, and devoted elite guards who would kill or die to ensure his anonymity and safety.

His power and control were only limited and thwarted by a powerful obstacle that seemed to have no solution that could be overcome. The obstacle was the same one that many of his predecessors were unable to overcome. It was the will and force and resources devoted to the ancient battle between good and evil.

His main enemy was the dying experiment in government known as Los Estados Unidos, the United States of America. Their founding fathers had created a unique system of liberty and minimal government that fueled creativity, entrepreneurism, freedom, exceptionalism and wealth never imagined by the philosophers and economists of old. They believed in rugged individualism and in the foolish idea that all men were created equal, and that they were endowed by their Creator with certain inalienable rights. They believed that these rights could not be bought, sold or removed.

Generations later, their offspring were infused with power of good and were responsible for stopping powerful evil nations from imposing genocide, order, governmental control and helpless equality on the masses. With blood, willpower and wealth, the forces of good conquered and destroyed those evil nations but then foolishly retreated, while funding the conquered nations' restoration instead of continuing and expanding their own dominion over them.

It was the power and ideology of the United States that was Benigno's greatest obstacle. While millions of her complacent citizens craved the enslaving mind altering drugs provided by Benigno and his colleagues, the US government spent billions of dollars on troops and technologies to stop the drugs from crossing their borders. While they touted free markets, they quashed Benigno's access to those markets and killed or imprisoned his customers and distributors. *What hypocrisy,* Benigno lamented. *Free people should be allowed the freedom to choose enslavement.*

All of that was about to change. Benigno was free of the constraints of the old order of Brujo Negros. He was about to transform thirteen of his disciples, instead of only one at a time as his elders had done throughout the ages. He was about to include two women into the fold. He was committing heresies that would have resulted in his painful death, if any of the remaining Brujos had the power to stop him.

None of them had the power he possessed. While the others had their hypnotic spells and potions, Benigno had more powerful spells, more powerful potions, and he also had the power of bullets. He systematically eliminated most of the Brujo Negros, stealing their secrets and sometimes keeping their disciples and turning them into his own.

Unbeknownst to the thirteen disciples, Benigno had ordered his own crack paramilitary guards to follow his entourage into the mountains. They followed at a safe distance, guarding their rear. Benigno carried a secure radio and a GPS locator so he could communicate in secret to his guards if necessary, and so far, his radio remained hidden in his pack.

Standing on a rock podium, Benigno patiently waited for his disciples to arrive at the sacred spot. One by one they straggled up to the meeting place. To his surprise, Luciana was the first to arrive.

Placing a small log in front of the rock podium, she then moved back several long steps. Her eyes blazed with fury fueled by her desperate thirst. Benigno sensed the battle that raged inside of her. *Yes, she wants to kill me for my water. I wonder if she will learn to control her rage.*

Staring at her with his cold pearl gray eyes, he felt her powerful presence. She had become the alpha among the others, blinded by her ambition and need to control. Overcoming this need would be her final internal battle and she would emerge either free or remain enslaved by her own mind.

Benigno remembered finding her when she was a young teenager, selling her body on the streets in an attempt to control the older men who paid her to satisfy their base cravings. She was hunted by the police for killing her stepfather after he abused her for years. Her mother was lost in her own affair with the bottle. Her mother was enslaved to the stupor of alcohol and was too weak to intervene. Luciana vowed never to be that weak and never to be controlled by men.

Luciana perfected her seductive craft in the back alleys of Buenos Aires and maneuvered her way up the chain to become a favorite of wealthy and powerful men. She derived intoxicating power from her abilities to manipulate and control these men, but her hatred of them sometimes exploded into violence. It was after one such violent explosion that Benigno found her, wandering blindly on the

Avenida del Libertador, several blocks from the five star Alvear Palace Hotel. Her hands were splattered with the dried blood of her last customer.

He had walked alongside her, gently speaking to her and slowly taking control of her mind with his hypnotic inductions. She followed him to his luxury vehicle and he took her to his mansion and estate in Palermo Chico. It was there that she began her apprenticeship into the Brujo Negro. Benigno taught her to control her violence, her pain, her mind, and to master the secret martial arts of the Brujos.

At first, he allowed her to use her seductive skills on him, letting her believe she was in control. Slowly, be began to introduce her to more exotic sexual dances, finally bringing her to her first orgasm and then pulling away when she craved more. He taught her the secret art of inducing her own orgasms using only her mind. She was an eager student of the Brujo pharmacopeia and she helped Benigno test his new concoctions on helpless peasants.

By the end of the year, Luciana was ready to join the other disciples for their advanced training. He turned her over to his lieutenants who taught her the intricacies of management and distribution of Benigno's drug empire. She learned the art of disguise and how to cross borders while carrying contraband. She learned how to bribe and blackmail officials in every South and North American

country she infiltrated. She especially loved to
blackmail powerful officials. Yet, her need for
control and her hatred of men continued to hold her
back.

Standing before him now, Luciana was breathing
hard, and her hatred toward him was at its pinnacle.
Her eyes betrayed her. Benigno knew this was her
final test. She would either tame the wild beasts
inside her or she would die in this cold and lonely
place. She both loved him and hated him, and
neither emotion was permitted if she were to ascend
to become the first Bruja Negra.

Turning his eyes away from her, Benigno heard and
then saw the next group of disciples climbing up to
the sacred place. Six more of them arrived together
in silence except for their heavy breathing. Delfina
Sosa was the other female disciple, and was the last
to climb over the boulders. Benigno noted that they
were all helping each other over the boulders.
Good, good, they are becoming as one.

Placing their logs at the base of the podium and
moving into a semi-circle, three of them stood on
the far side of Luciana and three took their places to
her left. Benigno's eyes were glowing as he
examined each of them in turn. Their hatred boiled
within them and Benigno fought against its force.
He would not signal the approval he felt.

Moments later, another disciple was climbing over
the boulders. Only Benigno's eyes followed his

movements until he recognized that it was Franco. *So, my special one, you did not give up.* Luciana noticed the flash of a smile on Benigno's face and she did not need to turn to know that it was Franco joining the others.

First placing his log on the pile, Franco was passing behind her when she felt a shift inside of her body. She was momentarily distracted from her hate as something else was happening to her, something she neither wanted nor invited. *What the hell was that?* she wondered.

Walking to the end of the semi-circle, Franco turned and faced Benigno. Their eyes locked. *What is this*, Benigno mused. *Where is his hatred?* Something else was out of place. *What happened to his burns? Is it a trick of the starlight? No. His skin is smooth and healed! Why are his eyes so different?*

Climbing over the boulders, the final five disciples were dragging themselves to join the others. Turning his eyes toward the new group, he examined their movements. *Yes, they too are becoming as one.*

One by one, they were placing logs on the pile. Two of them, walking to the end of the semi-circle, started to pass Franco, but he shifted his place to force them to stand to his left, resuming his place at the far end. The other three were lining up on the other side, all facing Benigno. All five were breathing rapidly, gulping the thin air into their burning lungs. All five were feeling boiling rage aimed toward their mentor.

Benigno inspected them with his eyes. *Yes, yes. Feel the rage for one last time.*

Waiting for them to get their breathing under control, Benigno's eyes glowed and he prepared himself for the next step in their initiation. This had never been done before. No other Brujo Superior had ever attempted to push more than one disciple at a time into the state of ascension. He was now about to take on thirteen. Benigno was in uncharted territory, but this only served to steel his resolve. They would remember him, and future Brujos would sing his praises. Losing himself in his pride was his only failing and he chastised himself for feeling it now.

Soon I will have thirteen Brujos spreading out over the world: First America, then Europe, Australia, Africa, India, Japan, Indonesia, Russia. Only those infernal Moslem countries will be spared, until I can find a way to get past their crazy Imams.

Momentarily distracted by his musings, he missed what was happening to his disciples.

Starting with the disciple next to Franco, the man began to tremble and his eyes rolled back into his head. Taking a deep breath, he flung his head back and his arms stretched outward from his sides.

Franco grasped the man's right hand as the next man in line began having the same reactions. Faster and faster, each one of the disciples was captured by the same phenomena. Franco was excited, *it's working!*

Luciana was struggling against this, but she too finally succumbed. *What is happening to me? What happened to my hate? What happened to my love for Benigno? What is this new feeling?*

As the force of their hatred evaporated, Benigno found himself falling forward into the vacuum left behind. Catching himself at the last moment, he looked up at his disciples. They were all facing him with their hands at their sides. *No. No! This is wrong. This is too soon. I haven't even started with them.*

Reaching into his pack, Benigno removed a large container of powder, sprinkling its contents on the logs in front of him. Removing another large vial, he poured a handful of a different powder into his hand. Raising his thick arms and fists above his head, he began singing the *Cantar Asención*. He deep baritone voice echoed off of the canyon walls.

Finishing the first verse, he threw the powder onto the logs. A fireball erupted, illuminating his disciples. Their shadows danced behind them in the darkness. Benigno was looking deranged in the firelight as he raised his arms once again, continuing the chant. Moving in front of the first

Chapter 14

disciple to his right, Benigno looked into his eyes. His eyes were clear and focused. There was no hatred. He felt only the cold, loveless, force of a Brujo Negro. *How can this be? He is already ascended.*

Stepping to his left, he repeated his examination of each of his disciples with the same result. Reaching Lucinda, she too emitted the cold, loveless force, and he sensed that she had lost her need to control, but there was something else he did not recognize. There was something deeper, darker, and more malevolent than anything he had ever experienced. He felt almost afraid while looking into her eyes. Tearing himself away from her gaze, he shook his body like a dog shedding water. Continuing left, he saw and felt the transition in each of his remaining disciples.

Finally standing in front of Franco, he began feeling the same discomfort he had felt with Luciana. The same deep, dark malevolence, but it was far stronger in this one. Looking into Franco's eyes was like looking into a black hole. Benigno felt unbalanced, dizzy, and afraid. Benigno felt himself both pulled into those eyes and repulsed by their malevolence. His thoughts were racing now. *What is happening to me? What is happening to all of them? I should never have attempted to transform so many at once. Maybe the old Brujos were correct. Maybe these thirteen have somehow merged and evolved into something beyond my understanding. What have I done?*

THE MENDOZA CONNECTION

His thoughts were shattered by the sound of distant gunfire, echoing off the mountain walls. As if controlled by one puppeteer, twelve disciples turned in unison toward the sound. Only Franco was staring back at him. Backing up slowly, Benigno disappeared into the darkness.

Chapter 15   Thursday, 13 hours earlier. Puente Del Inca

Waking up first, Carlos opened his eyes, surveying the room and listening. His body felt damp. It took a few seconds to remember where he was and why his head ached dully. *The casita; Antonia; Mendoza; too much tequila.* Turning his head to the right, he heard soft, rhythmical breathing coming from under a pile of blond hair. A rooster crowed three times, sending a chill down his naked brown body.

A faint light was drifting into the room through the curtained windows. Inhaling through his nose, he caught the intoxicating scent of Antonia mixed with the odor of burnt wood from the fireplace. Antonia had stolen the sheets, so Carlos was lying exposed on the double bed. His left arm was hanging over the edge of the mattress, as Antonia had nuzzled and pushed him to the edge sometime during the night.

Moving slowly, he began to sit up and turn so that his feet reached the floor. Trying not to wake her, he crawled out of the bed and stood up. Antonia stirred and mumbled something unintelligible, but kept sleeping. Ignoring the cold, Carlos walked to the window and peered through the curtains. The sky was turning a light gray.

Turning back to the room, he searched for his clothes, Finding his pants next to the bed, he slipped into them noiselessly. His shirt was inside the door, lying on top of Antonia's little black dress. Slipping his arms into his shirt sleeves, he picked up her dress and looked around the room for a closet. Seeing a pair of wooden doors with slats, he decided to try opening the one on the right, next to the bathroom door. Thankfully, it opened quietly. Reaching inside he found a hanger and hung up her dress. Turning around he searched the floor for his boots, but they were nowhere to be found.

Searching his memory was useless. *Jesus, where the hell are my boots?*

Resigning himself to walk barefoot, he gently unlocked and turned the brass doorknob of the sturdy front door. It opened silently, and he slipped outside. *Nice workmanship, José.* Quickly making a survey of the surroundings, Carlos noted that he could see through a passage into the courtyard of the hacienda. A light was on in the cocina. Starting toward it, his right big toe kicked something hard. Looking down, he saw it was one of his boots. Reaching down he turned it over and slammed the opening hard onto the ground several times in case any critters had taken up residence inside. Nothing fell out, so he slipped it over his left foot. Spinning around slowly, he resumed searching for his other boot.

Finding nothing, he began limping toward the light in the cocina. Finding his other boot at the edge of the walkway, he repeated the shaking and

177

slamming, before sliding his right foot inside. Buttoning his shirt, he walked through the courtyard into the kitchen. It was empty, but the room was filled with the aroma of rich coffee. A pot was simmering on the stove and a set of eight mugs were lined up on the counter.

Carlos filled a cup with the steaming dark liquid and blew on it a few times before attempting a sip. *Wow, that is some good coffee.* Taking the cup into the dining room, he saw that it was empty as well.

Walking to the front door of the hacienda, he reached out and turned the brass knob. It was unlocked, so he decided to go outside. It was getting brighter, and he could see his olive green SUV parked in the driveway. Walking over to it and unlocking the rear door, he reached inside and found his duffle bag. Removing a T-shirt and pair of sweats, he kicked off his boots and removed his jeans.

Once he was in the sweats and t-shirt, he found his socks and running shoes and laced them up. Looking around to ensure his privacy, he relieved himself next to the truck. Finding a jug of water, he downed a liter to slake his thirst.

After a few minutes of stretching, he checked his watch and began running down the driveway to the main road. His head was pounding more with each step and Carlos thought, *You deserve to hurt after last night.*

Lucas awakened with his face buried in a mound of hair. At first, he thought it was Bolo, but then he realized the hair smelled good, really good. Taking stock of his circumstances, he realized he was spooning next to a woman's naked body. In a flash of memory, he realized he was lying with Alícia.

A wave of conflicting emotions washed over him. A part of him wanted to stay exactly where he was, never letting go. Realizing he was erect, another part of him wanted a repeat of last night's tender lovemaking. His bladder was screaming for relief. Another part of him wanted to get started on their mission. His bladder won the conflict.

Untangling himself from Alícia, Lucas gently got out of the bed. Alícia never stirred. Walking quickly to the bathroom, he closed the door. Lifting the seat, he had to lean way over, one hand on the wall behind the commode and the other pushing down to aim the contents of his overfilled bladder into the commode, hoping the noised would not wake her. When he was finished, he put the seat down and washed his hands. Gently, he opened the door, and finding that Alícia had not moved an inch, he thought, *Wow, she is really out of it.*

Checking to make sure she was still breathing, Lucas thought briefly about returning to bed. Instead he found some new clothes neatly folded on a chair. Pulling on his pants and slipping into his boots, he stood up. Carrying the rest of his clothes, he stepped into the morning. It was light outside. Making a quick survey of his surroundings, he saw Ropes and Sparks crawling out of their casita. Walking toward them, he whispered loudly, "It's about time you two got up."

Looking at each other guiltily at first, the three men suddenly broke into wide smiles. Sparks was standing shirtless, holding a pile of clothing in his arms. He dressed quickly, finally hopping into his boots. Ropes was already dressed.

Looking at the clothing in his arms, Lucas realized he was also holding a dress. "Shit, shit, shit." Sneaking back into the casita, he quickly returned, buttoning up his shirt, and slipping into his vest.

Looking around, Ropes asked, "Where's Carlos?"

Lucas only shrugged. Turning toward Carlos' casita, He looked at the door for a few seconds, before deciding that knocking would not be a good idea. The three silently agreed to head to the cocina. Entering the courtyard, they found Carlos sitting in a chair with his feet up on the edge of the fire pit. Looking up at them, he growled, "It's about time, you slackers. Coffee is on the stove."

The three hurried inside, soon returning with the steaming beverages. Carlos made a show of looking at his watch and shaking his head. Muttering just loudly enough for them to hear, he said, "Pinche Gringos. It's seven o'clock already. We have to leave before eight. I'm going to grab a shower and meet you back here in thirty minutes, Okay?"

Standing up, Carlos hurried back to his casita, still shaking his head. The remaining three looked at each other while chugging their coffee. Watching Carlos walking away, Lucas waited until he was out of earshot before whispering, "Pinche Gringos, my ass." Carlos stopped suddenly and turned around. "I heard that." Turning toward the casita, he continued walking away.

Sparks spoke first, with an alarmed look on his face, asking, "Did he really hear you?"

"No, Sparks, he just knows me too well."

Lucas' showering woke Alícia, who was now sitting on the edge of the bed with a dazed look on her face.

Without telling her the details of their mission, he apologized again for having to leave and only told her that the mission could not succeed without him, and that was the reason he had to go, even though he wanted to stay.

As the four men exited their casitas in unison, all four women stood in the doorways of their respective casitas, watching the backs of the men walking away. The four women then looked at each other briefly, smiled awkwardly, and then closed and locked their doors and went back to sleep.

Examining Lucas' outfit, Carlos saw he was wearing a matching camouflage shirt, cargo pants, and vest. "She set out your clothes for you, didn't she?"

"How did you know?"

"Just a lucky guess," Carlos replied, turning away smiling to himself.

The men busied themselves with checking and arranging their gear. Searching the luggage area, Lucas said, "Wait a minute. We are missing rifles."

Leaving the barn, José quickly approached the men loading the gear into the back of Carlos' Land Cruiser. He was carrying an old green knapsack on his back, and four Colt LE6920 SOCOM rifles outfitted with Trijicon ACOG 4x32 scopes. He had one strapped to each shoulder and was carrying the other two in his hands.

Handing one of the rifles to Carlos, José shrugged and said "This was the best I could do on short notice. I also brought you 5.56 rounds instead of the .223s. I broke in the rifles and set the sights for you."

Looking at him with his mouth open in genuine surprise and appreciation, Carlos asked. "How in the world did you get these?"

José shrugged and said simply, "I know a guy, who knows a guy."

"Yeah, okay, I know. No questions."

Raising the rifle butt to his shoulder and peering through the scope, Carlos tested the weight and balance. Lucas and Ropes did the same with theirs. Sparks merely turned his over, admiring the fit and finish of his rifle. Letting the heavy knapsack slide off his shoulders, José set it inside the vehicle with a thump. Reaching inside the pack he said, "Here are twelve 30-round magazines, already loaded, plus the rest of the rounds in plastic cases. Are you sure you don't need me to come along? Maria has a long list of chores for me today."

Laughing softly, Lucas smiled at him. "I know. She already told me and made me promise to make you stay behind."

Dropping his shoulders in resignation, José frowned at Lucas. "Pinche traitor. I thought we were friends."

"We are, amigo, but she cooks better than you. And, as they say, if the momma ain't happy, ain't nobody happy." The rest of the men nodded in agreement.

"Look at you," José admonished them. "Four grown men with rifles and you are afraid of an old woman?"

Looking at each other and then back to José, Carlos and Lucas replied, "That's an affirmative."

Shaking his head at them, José answered, "Okay then, vatos." Pointing his finger at each of them in turn, he warned them, "You owe me one; each of you owe me one." Becoming more serious, he said, "Now get out of here."

Walking away, he suddenly stopped after a few steps. Turning around, he added, "Vaya con Dios."

"And you also, amigo," Lucas replied. *We still need to have our talk.*

Turning back to the vehicle, Lucas watched Carlos carefully wrap the rifles in blankets and miscellaneous clothing to protect them from each other. Carlos then slipped the rifles into two of the duffle bags. Dividing the ammunition and magazines into four piles, he added a pile to each of the four backpacks and zipped them up. Closing the back of his truck, he said, "Let's roll."

The men rode in silence for the next hour, lost in their own thoughts, up the winding road to Puente Del Inca. Breaking the silence, Sparks announced from the back seat, "According to the recording from the tracker, he left the airport after about two hours. He then traveled up this road until he was out of range. I don't know where he is now."

Ropes growled, "I have a pretty good idea where he is. If we're lucky, we will catch up to him soon, but we may be running out of time."

That was all Carlos needed to hear. Pushing down on the accelerator, he began driving maniacally up the mountain road. His passengers all tightened their seat belts.

In another hour, Carlos finally slowed the truck and pulled into the parking lot in front of the hosteria, The Hotel Puente Del Inca. It was a two story stone building with a green metal roof. There was only one other vehicle in the lot. Getting out of the vehicle, the four men stretched and the three passengers gave silent prayers of thanks for arriving safely. It was a cool 40 degrees and there was a brisk breeze in the thin air. There were piles of snow at the north edges of the building and on top of the north facing roof.

A rusted white pickup truck was bouncing and heading in their direction. The men tensed as it slowed and stopped a few yards away. There was only the driver, and the bed of the truck was piled high with bales of straw. Watching the men for a few moments, the driver turned off the engine, waiting until the shaking, clattering and sputtering stopped. Opening his door and stepping out of the truck, he limped around the door and approached the men.

Stopping a few meters away, he looked suspiciously at the four men. He was dressed in old jeans and a dirty, old red North Face parka. His skin was very dark and wrinkled. In a thick accent, he said, "Buenos dias. I yam lowking for Lucas."

Lucas stepped forward saying, "Buenos dias, I am Lucas."

Looking suspiciously at his camouflage outfit, he asked, "Are you a Federale?"

"A Federale? No. no. I am an Americano, tourista."

Grunting, he said, "Then I am Pablo Silva. Follow me in your truck." Turning around, he limped back to his truck and climbed in. It took him several tries to start the truck, but it finally sputtered into life. Making a wide u-turn, he drove up the road a kilometer, pulling behind a long building with stables and several open trailers. Several men were occupied throwing straw and hay into the stables.

Pulling up along side of the pickup, Carlos leaned out of his window and asked, "Where should I park my truck?"

The old man looked at him curiously and answered, in much better English this time, "We are not staying here. José said to load up two mulas and drive back down the road many minutes. If you want to speed things up, you can help me hook up the trailer." He pointed to one of the trailers.

Carlos and Ropes hooked up the rusty trailer while Lucas was speaking to Pablo, handing him an envelope. Slipping the envelope into his pocket, Pablo limped over to the stable and spoke to two of the men. The men went inside the stables, returning with two mules, which they loaded onto the trailer. Fastening the bridles to the front of the trailer, the men jumped down and climbed into the truck.

Coaxing his engine back to life, Pablo shouted, "Follow me." He started driving away without waiting.

Once everyone was back in the Land Cruiser, Carlos pulled out onto the main highway and began following the slow moving trailer. After driving about 25 kilometers at a maddeningly slow pace, the pickup slowed even more and turned right, down a rutted dirt road. They bounced slowly for another ten kilometers until the road ended, and the two muleteers jumped out of the pickup and led the mules off the trailer.

Pablo limped over to Carlos and said, "Let my men load up your gear; they know what they are doing."

Seeing Lucas nod, his three friends began unloading their gear from the back of their vehicle. Pablo was right. The muleteers loaded up the gear and several boxes of food for the mules, fastening everything down in a matter of minutes. When they were finished, Pablo turned to Lucas and asked, "Are you ready?"

"Let's go."

The muleteers led the mules down a narrow trail. Soon they were at the edge of the Rio Mendoza. There was an impossibly narrow and primitive wooden bridge that led across to the other side. Two ropes provided minimal security for the sides, and one was strung overhead.

The Rio Mendoza was fed by the Rio Horcones to the north and the Rio Tupungato from the south. During the spring melt, the waters poured off of the glaciers, and the river licked the tops of the banks. During the late summers, the runoff slowed and the river dried up to one-half its size, leaving behind sandy and rocky flats on each side that made walking easier. The centers of the rivers still raged, making the crossings dangerous.

Without stopping, the muleteers led the nervous mules onto the bridge, crossing over the raging river. Moving carefully, Lucas and the team followed, looking straight ahead, rather than down at the certain death below. Grabbing the upper rope, Sparks pulled himself along, his feet barely touching the wood below. *Don't look down. Don't look down*, he kept reminding himself.

Reaching solid ground, the men exhaled, not realizing they had been holding their breath. Despite his limp, Pablo followed the men across without touching any of the ropes. Arriving at the other side, he checked the lashings on the mules.

"Let them graze after about six hours, making sure they are hobbled, and let them rest a little, but not too much. Otherwise, you may not get them moving again. They will make their way back to the bridge if you let them go. They will not cross by themselves. When you return, do not attempt to lead them back to the other side, just cross over yourselves and drive back to the stables. We will retrieve them."

The muleteers crossed back over the bridge, and Pablo turned to follow them. At the edge of the bridge, he waved, "Vaya con Dios." They watched him limping across without difficulty.

Sparks muttered, "How does he do that?"

Lucas mused, "Practice."

When Pablo and his men were out of sight, Carlos removed the rifles and inserted loaded magazines, racking the slides and checking the safeties before handing them out. Each man now carried two spare magazines in pouches on their left hips. Behind the rifle magazine pouches, each of them carried their two spare handgun magazines. In their packs, they carried additional boxes of cartridges for the rifles and handguns. They holstered their handguns last. Once loaded up, the men shouldered their rifles and began walking rapidly. Each man took point for an hour and then traded positions.

Six hours and thirty kilometers later, Carlos, who was in point position at the time, signaled for a stop.

"This looks like as good a place as any. Let's rest and feed the mules."

Sparks opened the boxes of mule food, and removed the hobbles. Ropes fastened the hobbles to the front legs of the annoyed and protesting mules and let them graze on the meager grasses. Sparks threw some of the alfalfa and hay onto the ground in front of the mules. Carlos broke out packages of jerky, nuts and dried fruit, passing them around. The men ate in silence as they gazed up at the summit of Tupungatito volcano. The sun would be setting behind the Andes in an hour or so.

Lucas finally spoke. "Ropes, you take point next. We have to find the trail before it gets dark, otherwise, we may be too late." Staring off into the distance, Ropes merely grunted. He was the most experienced tracker of the group.

"I have spotted many different footprints," he offered. "I estimate ten to twelve are wearing flat sandals. They are traveling light. Behind them are a dozen or more footprints of a group wearing military style boots. The latter are likely carrying heavy packs. Given the urine patterns, there may be two or more women in the sandals group, unless there is one of them with a small bladder."

Looking at Ropes with new admiration, Sparks wondered to himself, *How does he do that?*

Carlos was down by the water, sucking the river water through a purifier into a two gallon collapsible jug. Sparks was feeding some alfalfa hay to the mules by hand. After each man drained their water bottles into their stomachs, Carlos refilled them with the filtered water. "Time to move, ladies."

Ropes removed the hobbles, handing them to Sparks to secure in the food boxes. Taking point, Ropes set a faster pace. As the sun was touching the tops of the mountains, Ropes pointed to a trail leading off to the west, toward the volcano. The trail steepened, and their pace slowed. The men were hyperventilating now, trying to inhale enough oxygen in the thin air to keep them going.

The sun set, but now the moon was already almost overhead. After a few more hours, Ropes stopped at a clearing. He found evidence of a recent fire and pieces of bloody aloe. "Someone got hurt." Sparks, looking down at one of his devices, exclaimed excitedly, "I've got him!"

The three men raised their rifles and scanned the area around them. Seeing this, Sparks knelt down, looking around himself anxiously. "The signal is

weak. It could be the battery, or he is far away."
Pointing to the volcano, he added, "He is in that
direction."

The men were energized by the news. "Break out
the coms," Lucas ordered. Unzipping a side pouch,
Sparks found and then handed out the earpieces.
Lucas added, "Unload the mules, except for their
food boxes. Everyone grab some grub, water,
ammo, and your sleeping bags. Stash the rest of our
gear behind those boulders. Let the mules go."

After the mules were unloaded, Ropes tuned them
around and slapped their haunches. The mules
began slowly moving back down the trail, retracing
their steps. It was Carlos who was now in point
position, and he set a brutal pace. They did not rest
for another two hours. The moon was getting lower
in the sky, and soon they would have to slow down
because of the darkness.

After the moon set, Ropes suddenly exclaimed,
pointing toward the volcano, "What the hell is
that?"

Looking up, the men saw a small dot of light,
flickering far in the distance, near the summit of the
volcano. Pulling out his high powered binoculars,
Carlos braced himself against a bolder and tried to
find the light. Adjusting the focus and holding his
breath, he stared through the lenses. After a few
seconds, he announced. "It looks like a fire, but the
color seems wrong."

Just then, Ropes saw a brighter flash, closer in, and they heard the sound of a bullet whizzing by over their heads by only a meter. "Hit the deck!" he shouted. As they were dropping to the ground, the blast of the gunfire reached their ears.

"That was close," he said. "That was a rifle; I estimate less than three hundred meters away." The men got up and started running forward in a crouch, their rifles raised. More gunfire erupted, the rounds hitting all around them. They fanned out as they pressed on quickly. After a hundred meters, they stopped, each finding some cover.

Suddenly, the side of the mountain was lit up with dozens of flashes, followed quickly by the sound of bullets striking all around them. The sounds of the rifle blasts reached them much faster this time.

Covering his head, Sparks was whispering, "Shit, shit, shit."

Lucas called out to Carlos, "Fire on the muzzle flashes, work your way from left to right. Ropes, shoot at the middle ones. I'll take the right side. Shoot and roll. Ready? Go!"

Dropping into a prone position, Carlos aimed upwards and waited for a flash. Seeing one, he steadied his aim and fired back three times. Rolling to his left, he heard a man cry out in pain.

Kneeling behind a small boulder, Ropes took aim and fired at the next flash from the middle, hearing a loud grunt. He shifted to the right on the other side of the boulder, taking aim again. The boulder was blasted by twenty or more rounds, near where he fired the first time. He loosed three more rounds in quick succession at the muzzle flashes. His ears were ringing now and he could not hear if his rounds connected.

Lucas found two targets on the right, firing on them before rolling further to the right. His previous position was peppered with dozens of rounds. Peeking out from the right side of a small boulder, he saw several more flashes coming from somewhere in the middle.

Suddenly he heard a single shot ring out from behind him, but higher up. A man in the distance screamed. Over the coms, he heard Sparks exclaim, "I think I got one!" Suddenly, a dozen rounds hit the top of the boulder where Sparks had been hiding.

"Sparks? Are you okay?

"I'm fine, Lucas, Shoot and roll, right?"

Far to his left, he heard Carlos fire a couple of rounds, hearing another man scream in the distance. Ropes fired again with the same result.

Whispering again over the coms, Sparks suggested, "Close your eyes for a few seconds, gentlemen, I'm going to light them up." He fired a flare overhead in the general direction of their attackers. The flare exploded over the heads of the enemy and slowly parachuted down, turning night into day.

"Carlos fired three more times in quick succession at three figures that were no longer hidden. All three flew backward as the rounds connected in their center chest cavities. Ropes and Lucas took out two more each, and Sparks' second single shot landed squarely in the middle of a man's face, dropping him instantly.

Carlos spotted two men running away and took out the one on the left. As he was getting the second man in his sights, he heard a shot and saw the man's head disappear in a cloud of pink mist.

"That'll teach him," Sparks said.

The flare flickered out. Waiting for several minutes, Lucas announced, "Test round," and fired blindly in the dark to see if anyone would fire back. No one did.

"Anyone see any movement?"

Three "No's" answered over the coms.

"Anybody hurt?"

195

Three more "No's"

"Okay, tactical reload if you haven't done so already." Only Sparks needed the reminder. He released the used magazine from his weapon and inserted a fresh one. As they waited, the men topped off their used magazines and inserted them into their pouches.

"Let's move up. Stay sharp. Sparks, come up here between me and Ropes."

"Okay boss," Sparks whispered, standing right behind Lucas. Lucas jumped and growled at him. "Don't ever do that!"

"Okay, boss." Sparks was secretly happy that he got the jump on Lucas.

The men moved up the rugged terrain. They eventually found twelve bodies. The men were all carrying AK-47s and were dressed in black fatigues. Each of them had a tattoo on their neck. One of them was the man in the leather jacket from the airport.

Reaching into his pocket, Sparks pulled out his tracking device and shut it off. Turning away he started vomiting. It was his first kill and once he saw the mangled bodies, it was not what he expected. His video games did not prepare him for the horror he now felt.

Lucas put his arm around his shoulder, whispering, "It was us or them. You probably saved thousands of lives today. Try to remember that. When you are ready to talk, we will be there for you." Sparks could only nod. Knowing he needed to get Sparks out of his head, he gave him a task to perform. "Help me get their guns." They gathered up the AKs and piled them behind a boulder on the trail.

Looking up at the volcano, Lucas saw that the fire was still burning in the distance. "Let's get some rest. I'll take first watch."

Not needing any encouragement, the tired men pulled out their sleeping bags and set them on their self inflating mattresses. The two of the men were asleep in minutes. Sparks stayed awake, staring at the stars, and talking with his God for many hours.

Lucas found a good lookout spot and settled in, keeping watch over his brave friends.

Chapter 16   Friday. Jesús Morales – Portals

Jesús awakened in darkness, struggling to get his bearings. Listening past the buzzing in his ears, he heard the sound of water dripping. Remembering where he was and sitting up slowly, his body reminded him of his age. Each of his joints was checking in with pops and cracks and twinges of pain. The noises echoed off the tunnel walls. Sitting up on the edge of the chest, he realized that he was getting used to living in a lava tube, but he missed the sunlight and was worried about his burro. *Soon, Enrique will be checking on me and he will be upset. He will have no idea where I am, poor boy.*

Sitting in the blackness, Jesús knew he was a happy man, for many years ago he had learned the true secret of happiness. His Abuélo started teaching it to him when he was a young boy, but his mind could not fully understand it until he was in his mid twenties. His brain had to finish the process of pruning neurons and adjusting its chemistry before he was capable of comprehending and applying the secret.

He remembered walking with his Abuélo, seeing that there was so much unhappiness in the big cities he visited. During one trip, his Abuélo taught him to look beyond the surface, seeing people who had amassed great material wealth who smiled on the outside, but their eyes betrayed them. Their eyes revealed their inner turmoil and dissatisfaction. Because of their simple peasant clothing, the wealthy people would ignore their presence. He and his Abuélo were invisible to them and he could listen to them and observe them unnoticed.

Jesús overheard their conversations but secretly observed their body language that revealed so much more. He learned that the unhappy ones could be materially rich or materially poor. His Abuélo taught him that both were often driven by the same two faulty beliefs and by the one hidden emotion. The two faulty beliefs seemed related. I will be happy if… and I will be happy when…

The hidden emotion was fear. They were driven by their fear of losing what they had and by their fear of not getting what they pursued. It was as if they could never say, "This is enough."

One of the most important lessons he learned was that happiness is a decision. No matter his circumstances, he could choose to be happy.

Jesús began his morning ritual of gratitude.

Thank you for my feet and all my toes.
I am blessed.
Thank you for my legs.
I am blessed.
Thank you for my manhood.
I am blessed.
Thank you for my working bowels.
I am blessed.
Thank you for my hands and all my fingers.

I am blessed.
Thank you for my arms and shoulders.
I am blessed.
Thank you for all my senses.
I am blessed.
Thank you for my mind.
I am blessed.
Thank you for the water that quenches my thirst.
I am truly blessed.
I have enough.

The pain from his bladder wrenched him from his ritual. Standing up to a standing ovation of popping and cracking from his joints, he shuffled over to the table. Having spent what he estimated to be two days in this small room, he knew where everything was even in the darkness.

Reaching out he found the striker with his right hand, and the lamp with his left hand. Feeling the weight of the lamp and shaking it, he knew it was only one third full. Feeling the wick and finding it still damp, he closed his eyes and scraped the striker near the wick. The sparks were too bright and he did not want to hurt his eyes. Squinting at the lamp, he saw that it was lit. Replacing the globe, and opening his eyes, he felt joy that the room and its meager contents reflected a warm yellow glow.

Carrying the lamp in front of him, he shuffled down the tunnel until he could smell his makeshift latrine. Holding onto a wall for support, he set down the lamp and coaxed his bladder into action. When the stream finally flowed, he was happy at the relief, and happy that it was almost clear. When he was finished, his bladder pain was replaced with a different urge from his bowels.

Opening the lid of the small box that previously contained the carne seca, but was now filled with its digested and processed end result, Jesús tried to breathe through his mouth. Leaning his back against the wall, and sliding down, he squatted over the open and odiferous box. Despite the pain in his bowels, his movement came slowly and painfully. *I need some vegetables soon.* Tearing off a piece of his old clothing that sat in a pile next to the box, Jesús cleaned himself. Struggling to stand erect, Jesús used the wall for assistance as he shuffled back to his new home.

Washing his hands and face in the basin he felt much better. Reaching into the trunk, he removed a box of the dried meat and began making his simple stew. While it was heating over the lamp, he tested himself to see if he remembered the contents of the book. Jesús believed he understood all but the last few chapters.

Something about the chapter on Arca Deus bothered him. Closing his eyes, he searched his memory. The last time he met with Enrique, the boy seemed so excited about some of his private studies. *What was it he was talking about? He went on and on about something called quantum physics, and existing in two places at once. He kept talking about some cat. What did he call it? Oh yes, Schrödinger's cat. Supposedly, it was some great puzzle. The cat was in a box, but was it alive or dead? Enrique said it was both alive and dead. When you opened the box, your observation caused it to be either alive or dead in the present reality.*

Suddenly, Jesús' eyes opened. *That's it! That is the reason for the peculiar mixture of certain plants. The hallucinogenic mixture would give a person an out-of-body experience in which you could observe yourself. You would be there and not there. You could be in two places. You might even have the ability to traverse great distances.*

Picking up the book, he turned to the final pages. *Perhaps I missed something. Where is the doorway?* Jesús had not ventured past this room. His body had told him he needed to rest and he now felt much better, but he could not stay here. He was running out of lamp oil and food. No one had come to replenish them. He could find no more answers in the book.

Returning to the chest, Jesús removed the small leather backpack and one unopened box of food. Turning back toward the table, he debated what to take and what to leave behind. Carefully placing the small bottles of powder into the backpack, he then added the bowl and one of the candles. *I will need the flint and striker, but there is only one set.*

THE MENDOZA CONNECTION

If someone else like me ends up here, they will need light.

He remembered seeing a small rock by the water basin, and shuffled over to retrieve it. Using the sharp edge of the rock, he was able to break the flint in half. Placing one half of the flint in his backpack, he returned the other half to the box. Holding the striker blade in his hand, he knew he would be unable to break it in half. Looking down at the table, he suddenly realized that someone could use the sword as a striker if they needed to. He did not think he would need the sword himself, so he added the striker blade to the backpack.

The bottle of mezcal was now sadly empty and the worm had been digested last night. Filling the bottle with water, he capped it tightly and added it to his pack. Drinking as much water from the basin as he could stomach, Jesús turned back to the table and lit one of the candles. Taking one last look around the room, he extinguished the oil lamp. Holding the candle in front of him, he began walking slowly up the unexplored tunnel.

****

Running as fast as he could in the star light, Benigno found himself tripping and sometimes falling on the rugged trail. The gunfire in the distance seemed to be getting closer. He had no idea who had confronted his security force, but the firefight seemed fierce. Stopping to catch his breath and turning around, he saw a bright flare arcing through the sky, followed by multiple retorts.

Standing there until the flare died out, he realized there was no more gunfire. Either his men were successful or they were dead. Either way, he had to keep going because he had apparently lost control of his disciples. He was particularly worried about Franco and Luciana. There was something about their eyes that frightened him.

Reaching into the pack for his radio, he turned it on and called for the leader of his security force. There was no response. He tried several more times with the same result. Reluctantly, he turned it off. Crouching down, he turned the dial on his flashlight until it reached the red light setting. Unzipping a side compartment in his backpack, he removed his copy of the map given to him just before his mentor died. Turning on the red light, he examined the map and his surroundings. There were symbols on the map that he did not understand, but the trail seemed to lead to some kind of doorway.

When his mentor was dying, Benigno stayed with him, trying to comfort him, but also trying to get his mentor to reveal his secrets. Benigno was angry with him because his mentor had refused to share his secret knowledge with Benigno during the past two years. Elisandro was supposed to pass his knowledge onto Benigno, but for some reason he kept Benigno hanging. The old man was babbling something about some sorcerers from the stars. He said they left behind some powerful objects deep inside some volcanoes. In his last moments, he gave the map to Benigno, but died before explaining the meaning of the symbols. All he knew was that something inside the volcano, something beyond an entrance, would give him ultimate power.

All Benigno knew was that he had to say on this trail until he found some kind of entry. Returning the map to his backpack, he stood up and plowed ahead. *I will find it in spite of you, you old bastard.* Stuffing coca leaves into his mouth and hyperventilating to get oxygen into his bloodstream, Benigno started running up the trail.

After an hour of running, he collapsed on the trail. Leaning against a boulder, and gulping air into his lungs, he peered into the darkness. The sky was exceptionally clear because of the altitude, and the starlight was sufficient for him to see through the darkness. I must be close, because the map ends here. *Where is this entrance, Elisandro? Were you lying to me?*

Feeling desperation, Benigno stood up and slowly turned around 360 degrees. He found nothing. Swearing under his breath, he tried slowly turning around once more. When he was almost finished with the circle, he saw a flash out of the corner of his eye to the right. Looking straight at it he could see nothing, but he walked forward anyway. In the shadows, he could see a large outcropping of rock. Moving closer, he began to see stars. *How can this be?* Continuing to walk forward, Benigno saw it was a reflection of the stars in the sky.

A few steps forward, Benigno realized he was looking into a large mirror in the side of the rock outcropping. *This is it! Elisandro spoke of a mirror in the rock. He was not delusional, after all.*

Grasping the mirrored rock, Benigno pushed and pulled, but to no avail. Taking a step back, he contemplated the mirror and thought to himself, *this must be an entrance, but how does it open?*

Grasping the shiny rock once again, he tried turning it to the left. It would not budge. He tried turning it to the right, and he felt it move slightly. Taking a deep breath, and using all of his strength, he again tried pushing and turning it to the right. The mirror began to move along the track at its bottom. Pushing harder, he was able to roll it enough for him to step inside. Removing his flashlight from his pack, and pressing the button, the red light illuminated a narrow shelf at the bottom, but only darkness beyond.

Without hesitating, Benigno stepped inside. Sitting down on the shelf, he let go of the mirrored rock. It rolled back into place. Benigno turned the dial on his flashlight until it emitted a bright white beam of light. He saw that he was sitting on the edge of a downward sloping tunnel. Realizing he had nothing left to lose, he pushed off from the shelf and began sliding down the tunnel. After a few seconds, he found himself sitting at the bottom.

Moving the beam of his flashlight, he saw he was at a crossroads of some kind of tunnel. *This looks like a lava tube.* To the right to tunnel seemed to drop off. To the left, the tunnel rose at a slight incline. Closing his eyes, he tried to sense which direction to take. He thought he felt a slight pull to the left. Standing up, he began running up the tube to the left.

****

Running up the trail, Franco was frantically searching for signs of Benigno. The crafty Brujo had somehow escaped into the darkness and was running away from him. *He is afraid of me now. Wait until he sees what I can do to him. I will show him my power. I will make him reveal any remaining secrets before I slit his throat. Soon I will be the one in control.*

Luciana, running a few paces behind, was struggling to breathe and trying to fight her own body. *Why am I following Franco? Why can't I control my mind? What has he done to me?* She felt terrified by the sounds of gunfire, but she was more terrified the loss of control of her own mind and body.

Franco shouted to her, "There he is!" He was pointing to a place near the base of the volcano.

207

Looking up, Luciana thought she saw a reddish light far into the distance. She needed to rest, but her feet kept moving her up the trail behind Franco. The light disappeared.

****

Taking a long drink from the mezcal bottle of water, Jesús realized that he had consumed almost three quarters of the bottle. He had promised himself he would turn back at this point. *Just a little further,* he thought.

Holding the candle in front of him, he continued up the lava tube. A few moments later, the tunnel widened. Lowering the candle in front of him, he slowly shuffled forward, fearing that there might be a hole in the floor. Raising the candle, he noted the height of the ceiling had not changed. Continuing a few more steps forward, he began to see the outline of something in front of him. A few more steps, and it became clearer.

In the middle of the tunnel was a large, vertical rectangular object. It stood like a monolith in the middle of the room but did not reach the ceiling. It was held up at the bottom by a stone foundation. Approaching the object, he saw that it was almost a meter wide, and it was surrounded on both sides by square stone tiles. The top of the object appeared to rise up more than two meters tall.

Each of the tiles on the side held an embossed symbol. At first he thought they represented some type of graph. Upon closer examination, he thought they might be outlines of different landscapes or mountains. At the bottom of each tile was a circular opening. Jesús walked all the way around the object, and saw that it was only a few inches thick. Holding the candle in front of him, he searched the rest of the room.

To the right of the object, was a smaller object. Jesús thought that it looked like some type of musical instrument. It stood more than a meter tall. At the bottom was a square metal cube, perhaps two thirds of a meter wide on each side. Fastened to the back of the cube was a long tube, rising straight up. On the top of the tube was a brass cap with a small ring. Attached to the ring was a thin cable extending down to the middle of the top of cube.

Setting the candle on the floor, Jesús grasped the long upright tube in his left hand, as if he was playing a one string bass fiddle, and with his right hand, he pulled the cable and let go. The room was filled with a melodic sound that reverberated for several seconds. He plucked it a few more times, as the vibrations seemed soothing and the whole room seemed to vibrate in harmony.

Setting it down and continuing to explore the room, he saw that the walls of this room were different somehow. Instead of the melted lava, the walls seemed shinier. Tapping on them, Jesús realized that they were metallic. *Maybe that was why the sound reverberated so much.* He could not tell if this was a natural or man-made room.

****

Benigno noticed that the tunnel was widening, and there was a large monolithic object in front of him. Shining his flashlight around the room, he stood at the entrance, breathing deeply. The walls reflected the light as if they were metallic. Next to the central object was a metal box with a long tube rising out of its back. In a far corner, was a stone table with several objects sitting on top. Walking over to the table, he saw four small bottles, each containing some type of powder, and each a different color. There was a metal bowl and several larger bottles. In the back was some type of lamp and another large bottle. Next to it was a wooden box.

Flashing back to Elisandro's final words, he remembered him saying,

Colors of four will open the door.
A pinch of each and take no more
Hold the key and one will stay
Through the door, the other may

Benigno thought at the time that Elisandro was delusional, and a bad poet, but now he realized Elisandro was not just babbling, but was giving him some final message, some key to something spectacular. *The four bottles must be the colors of four, but where is the key and where is the door?*

Opening one of the larger bottles, he sniffed the contents. It was odorless. Pouring some of the liquid on to his fingers, he cautiously tasted it. I tasted like stale water. Opening the box, he saw it contained a metal tube and a short blade. Sticking out from under the box was a piece of parchment. Pulling it out, he pointed the flashlight and saw that it was filled with symbols or drawings.

Benigno recognized three of the drawings as depictions of plants and cacti with powerful medicinal attributes. He did not recognize one of the plants. The last drawings showed a figure drinking from a bowl followed by an image of two figures standing in front of a jagged circle with a spiral in the center.

Unable to contain his curiosity, Benigno opened the small bottles and placed a pinch of powder from each of them into the bowl. Adding some of the water, he swirled the mixture with his finger. Licking his finger, his tongue tingled with the bitter taste. *I wish I had a peasant to test this on first.* Hesitating a few moments, he finally raised the bowl to his lips and drank. Swallowing the mixture, he felt a tingling in his mouth and throat.

****

Scrambling up the trail, Franco realized that he may have gone too far. He could not find any more footprints from Benigno. Looking back toward the base of the cinder cone, he sensed that they were too far down. *We need to go higher up.* Turning to their left, Franco began ascending up the loose gravel on all fours. Luciana turned and followed him closely.

"There they are!" Franco shouted, pointing down in front of him. Fresh tracks could be seen even in the early morning light. Moving faster, they reached the end, standing in awe before the mirrored rock.

Franco somehow knew what to do. Grabbing the edge on the left, he pulled, and the shiny rock rolled to the right. "Get my flashlight, Luciana," he commanded.

Without hesitating, she reached into his pack and found the light. Holding the mirrored rock open with his back, Franco took the light and shone it into the darkness. Seeing the shelf and shaft beyond, he sent Luciana in ahead. Hearing her sliding down the tunnel, he realized she had stopped after a few seconds. Taking a deep breath, he followed her, letting the rock roll back into place.

****

Far ahead, Benigno pointed the beam from his flashlight around the room. *Where is the key and where is the door?* The walls were smooth and

212

almost shiny, but nothing looked like a door. He walked around the two objects in the center of the room, shining his light from top to bottom. Looking closer at the metal box, he saw the metal cable extending from the center of the box to the top of the metal tube. Pushing at the edge of the box with his foot, he saw that it moved easily. Picking it up, he examined the box to see if there was some opening. Maybe there's a key inside. Shaking it, he did not hear anything moving inside, but the cable started vibrating. A clear tone emanated from the box, and the walls echoed back.

Shaking his head in confusion, Benigno set the box down and turned the beam onto the larger object. Examining the structure more closely, he saw that it was surrounded by small embossed tiles. There were six tiles on each side and each tile had a small, irregular hole at the bottom. Cautiously, he touched the tiles and tried to move them. They were solidly attached to the large object. The face of the object was some type of dull metal panel almost two meters tall. Tapping the metal panel with his finger revealed nothing helpful to him.

Walking around the monolithic panel, Benigno frowned. *It is like a door to nowhere, standing in the middle of a room. Is this the door Elisandro was talking about? If it is a door, how do you open it, and why? It doesn't go anywhere.*

Turning back to the box, he reached out and plucked the cable. A beautiful sound filled the

213

room and the box seemed to vibrate. Examining the cable more closely, he saw it was attached to the top of the tube with a metal cap and ring. Reaching up, his fingers examined the cap. The cap was not round, but was shaped irregularly. Suddenly, his mind made the connection. *The cap must fit into the holes in the tiles! The whole box and tube is a key.*

Benigno began to feel dizzy and nauseated, and his eyes were losing focus. The walls of the room looked like they were melting. Looking down at his hands, his skin appeared to be moving, and his hairs were dancing. *Oh no, I'm tripping on drugs! Those powders were some kind of hallucinogens.* Benigno knew he needed to stay calm to avoid the paranoia the drugs could cause.

Stay focused. What was I just thinking about? Oh yes, the box is the key.

Placing the flashlight on its base, so that the beam shot upward, Benigno stepped forward and picked up the box. He felt like it was moving in his hands as if it were alive. Feeling his body shudder, he sensed he was losing control. Closing his eyes, he began seeing brilliant flashes of color. He felt like he was floating.

Quickly opening his eyes, he realized he was now looking down at himself from across the room. He was having an out of body experience. His mind was both outside his body and inside his body at the same time. He had become like two twin beings,

214

each seeing the world from a different perspective, each able to move separately, but his mind was one with both. The Benigno holding the box could now see the Benigno floating a few meters away. Surprisingly, neither one felt frightened.

Raising the box, Benigno inserted the brass end into the hole in one of the tiles. Plucking the cable, the entire room resounded with a beautiful, clear tone, and the box vibrated in his hands. The large metal panel began to vibrate at the same frequency. Benigno was also floating behind himself, watching and listening. The panel began to shimmer and swirl with a multicolored light that quickly faded and became transparent. Peering through the panel, the Benignos were looking into another room.

Standing in the other room was an old man in a white robe, staring back at them with a look of fear on his weathered face.

Chapter 17   Saturday. Unto the Breach

The sky was just beginning to lighten before the coming dawn. Carlos was standing between several boulders so that he could keep watch in all directions, but his body was hidden from most approaches. He was taking the last watch, the one that was often hardest. His three companions were sleeping soundly after the long hike and the harrowing battle the night before. He and Lucas had a quick conference last night, deciding that it would be safer to continue up the trail in daylight, even though they might miss apprehending their quarry. They had no idea how many more armed men there might be up ahead.

Drinking deeply from his water bottle, Carlos was suddenly overcome with the need to relieve himself. Taking one more look around him in all directions, he walked a few meters away from his post and unzipped his pants. In the quiet pre-dawn, the sound of his urination was almost deafening.

As he was finishing, Carlos began to feel very tired. *What is going on? I can barely stand up.* The tired feeling was being replaced by something else, something almost sexual. He began feeling an intense desire that was totally out of place in this camp. He felt a touch on his neck. Trying to turn around, he realized he was paralyzed and could not move. Something was now touching his shoulders and he wanted to turn and defend himself, but he was helpless.

A dark shape began to move in front of him. It was a beautiful woman in a black robe. Her scent was intoxicating. Looking into the dark eyes of the Bruja, Delfina Sosa, he found himself drawn deeply into her spell, with an overwhelming desire to possess her. He wanted to reach out to her, to disrobe her, to throw her down on the ground and make passionate love to her.

All he could do was stare into her eyes, and then there was blackness.

There was a sound in the distance, "Carlos!"

Who is calling my name?

"Carlos!"

Why is he hitting me?

"Carlos, wake up!"

Fluttering his eyes open, Carlos saw the face of Lucas looking down at him. The sky was intensely bright behind Lucas. *What is going on? Why am I lying down?*

Suddenly alarmed, Carlos tried to sit up, but something was holding him down. Looking down, he saw Lucas' hand on his chest.

"Don't try to sit up just yet. Carlos, do you know who I am?"

Looking confused, Carlos answered, "Of course I know who you are. You're Lucas. Now get the fuck off of me."

Rolling back on his heels, Lucas stood up and reached out a hand to Carlos, helping him sit up. Sparks and Ropes were behind Lucas, staring at Carlos with concerned looks on their faces.

Rubbing the back of his head, Carlos asked, "What the fuck, did I fall asleep? What time is it?

Quickly reaching for his sidearm, Carlos felt relief that it was still there. Looking around him, he saw his rifle next to him and that he was sitting between the boulders of his post. The sun was high in the sky. The back of his head was hurting badly.

"It is 0800, and we have been trying to wake you for over an hour." Lucas was looking down at him, but appeared more worried than angry. "What happened to you? You have never fallen asleep on your watch."

Carlos stared at the ground in front of him and tried to focus on what happened last night. Closing his eyes, he tried to think back at the last thing he could remember.

"I was taking a leak, and suddenly I felt overwhelmingly tired. I remember suddenly not being able to move."

Thinking hard, *What happened next?* Struggling to focus, Carlos began to remember. "There was a beautiful woman." Opening his eyes and looking around fearfully, he asked, "Where is she?"

The other three men looked at each other with a mixture of surprise and concern.

Turning back to Carlos, Lucas whispered, "Carlos, there is no woman here. I found you collapsed on the ground and could not wake you." *He actually looks frightened. What is going on, I have never seen him look this way."*

Ropes chimed in, "I found a lot of tracks headed back down the mountain. They were sandal tracks and they went right by here. One set led right up to here and then went back to the trail. It could have been a woman." Looking at Lucas, he added, "I could not tell if she was beautiful."

"Jesus, guys, I'm so sorry. I could have gotten us all killed." Regaining control and suppressing the fear, Carlos' face was now reddening with embarrassment and anger at himself.

Looking thoughtfully at Carlos, Lucas replied, "I think you had, and somehow survived, an encounter with a powerful Brujo or maybe a Bruja. I have heard of their ability to hypnotize people, but this seems to be something more powerful and sinister. I do not understand why they didn't kill you or all of us." Looking at the others, he continued, "Maybe they couldn't risk trying it on all four of us, or maybe they wanted us alive."

"Christ, Lucas, I couldn't move. I couldn't defend myself. In fact, all I wanted to do was seduce her."

Nodding thoughtfully, Lucas said, "Well, frankly, Carlos, that is not out of character for you. Maybe he or she preyed upon your weakness. She sensed it and used it against you."

Interested now, Ropes asked, "Well did you?"

"Did I what, Ropes?"

"Did you seduce her?"

Staring at Ropes for a few moments while searching his memory, he shook his head slowly and replied, "Unfortunately, I have no idea. I think I just passed out."

Smiling now, Ropes confessed, "Well that has happened to me a few times. I just didn't think it ever happened to you, Romeo."

Changing the subject, Lucas asked, "How are you feeling? Is anything broken?"

Making a quick survey of his body, Carlos replied, "Nothing is broken, but I must have fallen on my head. The back of my head is really sore."

"Well, I didn't find any blood, but try to stand up."

Sparks chimed in, "If you feel nauseated, let me know. You might have a concussion."

Grabbing his rifle for balance, Carlos stood up and looked around. Pulling out his water bottle, he took a long drink. "No nausea, just a headache."

Standing on one of the small boulders, Sparks was now searching the landscape through his binoculars. "The trail looks clear in both directions. We are safe from beautiful women."

Lucas tried to suppress a smile, but Ropes guffawed loudly.

Carlos groaned to himself, *Oh great. Here it comes. They're all going to get their digs in now.*

"I have to take a leak. I'll be right back."

Calling out after him, Ropes said, a little too loudly,

"Better check for crabs."

Snorting, Sparks elbowed Ropes, and whispered, "Good one."

Slinging his rifle, Carlos walked a few paces away from the group. As he began to relieve himself, he could not help checking himself a little more carefully than usual. Finding nothing amiss, when he was finished, he shook himself off. Pulling a small plastic bottle from one of his dozen pockets, he squeezed a few drops of the disinfectant into his hands and washed them vigorously.

Looking down thoughtfully, he remembered Ropes remark. Pouring a few more drops into his hands, he lowered them and washed his other appendage for good measure, and zipped up. Exchanging the bottle of disinfectant with a smaller plastic container, he shook four ibuprofen tablets into his hand, popping them into his mouth. Finishing the water in his bottle, he transferred the empty water bottle into his pack and found a fresh one, slipping it into his thigh pocket.

Giving Lucas a reassuring look, he said, "I'm good to go."

Looking carefully at Carlos, Lucas decided to accept his self assessment. "Okay, ladies. Ropes, you take point. Sparks, you take second, then Carlos you take third. I'll bring up the rear. We eat on the trail." Checking his watch, he announced. "It is 0830 and we need to get moving."

They rolled up their sleeping gear, stuffing it into their packs, checking the camp for any dropped items. Ropes stuffed a power bar into his mouth and took a drink from his camelback. All four men performed chamber checks and mag checks. Lucas noted approvingly that Sparks had started first, and had even checked his sidearm. Lucas commanded, "Stay sharp, all eyes and ears."

Ropes began pumping up the trail, his rifle at the ready position. One by one, the men followed him in line, adjusting to his pace. Every few minutes, Lucas stopped, and using his compact binoculars, searched the trail behind them.

At 0930, Ropes stopped suddenly, raising his fist into the air. The men each dropped to a knee taking up defensive positions, each one pointing their rifles in a different direction. Ropes pointed to his ear, and the men activated their com units. He whispered into his mic, "Com check." The other three quietly acknowledged him.

"I smell wood smoke, but can't see anything. The breeze is katabatic, so it must be coming down the mountains and rolling here from the other side of these boulders." Slinging his rifle, Ropes began quietly climbing up and over the boulders. Near the top, he went prone, crawling slowly forward.

Lucas saw him pause near the top and slowly survey the other side. Ropes announced, "No movement, no bogies. Sparks, come on up."

Slinging his rifle, Sparks followed him to the top, mimicking his movements. Joining the surveillance, Sparks looked around through his rifle scope and confirmed, "I got nothing." Moving into crouches and unslinging their rifles, Ropes went left and

Sparks went right. Carlos and Lucas watched them disappear, waiting tensely for several minutes. Finally, Ropes announced, "All clear. Move up." Keeping watch to the rear, Lucas sensed that Carlos was climbing over the boulders behind him.

Reaching the top, Carlos checked in all directions and signaled to Lucas to come up. Slinging his rifle, Lucas soon joined Carlos and they both moved forward onto the small plateau. Ropes was already at the far end of the plateau, searching the ground. Sparks was on one knee at the edge on the right, looking up the trail through his rifle scope.

Walking over to a small fire pit, Lucas reached down and felt for heat. He wondered, *Where the heck did they find wood up here?* The coals were still hot, and there was a thin wisp of smoke dancing in the breeze. Walking to the up windward side of the fire, Lucas unzipped and urinated into the coals. The liquid sputtered and boiled, sending a cloud of steam into the thin air. The thought came to him uninvited, *Only you can prevent forest fires.* He smirked at the irony. There were no trees around for fifty kilometers.

Ropes' voice was coming in over the coms, "I found three sets of sandal tracks. They are headed up the volcano. One looks like it could be a woman. Maybe it's your girlfriend, Carlos."

Having had enough of their teasing, Carlos replied, "When we catch her, I'll hold her down for you,

Ropes. That's the only way you're going to get any action."

"Well, well, Carlos. It's nice to have you back," Ropes countered.

Checking his watch, Lucas noted that it was 1045. "Ropes can you follow the tracks on this rock?"

"Lucas, I'm hurt. Do you really have to ask?"

"Okay then, let's get moving. Carlos, take second and look for anything unusual."

"There's nothing but unusual on this godforsaken trail, Lucas, but I'll do my best."

"Sparks, are you okay bringing up the rear?"

Standing up, Sparks answered, "Wilco, boss."

Ropes was already moving forward up the trail, with Carlos a few paces behind him. Within minutes, the men were hyperventilating, sucking out the meager oxygen from the cold, thin air. Every few dozen meters, Ropes and Carlos would stop and search the rocky ground carefully. After another half hour of this stop and go pace, Lucas saw Ropes waving Carlos forward.

"It looks like one set of tracks took a sharp left here. The other two seem to go straight ahead. Let's split up. I'll take the single track."

Whispering over the coms, Lucas warned, "Be careful. It could be an ambush. Sparks and I will stay here until we hear from you."

Brightening at the prospect of a rest, Sparks sat down on a small lava boulder, sucking down water from his camelback. While he was waiting, he munched on a sugary trail bar, keeping his eyes on the rear. Lucas found another small boulder a few meters away. The top was pocked-marked and rough, with many sharp edges. Pulling out a low carb, high protein bar, he thought, *I'm getting too old for this.*

Looking up at the summit of Cerro Tupungatito, Lucas squinted at the developing cumulonimbus clouds coming from the windward side out of the west. *We're going to need some shelter if it starts lightning.* Breaking into his musings, Carlos' voice came over the coms. "Ropes, they stopped after a few hundred meters and then turned left, headed in your direction."

Ropes replied, "I'm just picking up their trail. They are all headed up to that steep cinder cone, the one with the long mounds that flow down the mountain into the valley. Lucas, do you copy?"

"Copy that. We're heading up."
Groaning, Sparks stretched his lanky frame and adjusted his pack. Lucas was already moving up the trail. Taking one last look to the rear, Sparks began

moving upward. Checking his watch, Sparks noted it was past 11:15 and the sun was beginning its descent into the west. Ugly dark bottomed clouds were building ominously on the other side of the Andes.

Breathing rapidly, as the air continued to thin, and the incline steepened, Sparks found himself counting his exhalations to develop a rhythm. Walking for twenty rapid breaths and then resting for five breaths, he noticed he was able to keep pace with Lucas, who seemed to be maintaining the same rhythm. The lava rocks underfoot were small and loose, causing his boots to slowly slide backwards with each step. *Damn, this is like going up a down escalator,* he complained.

It took them almost fifteen minutes to catch up to Ropes and Carlos. Turning off their coms, the men found places to sit facing each other in a rough circle. Pulling their spare water bottles out of their packs, they each sucked down a liter of cold water. Turning to stuff the empty bottle into his pack, Sparks saw a flash of light coming from the base of the cinder cone.

"Incoming!" he shouted as hit the dirt face down, covering his head with his arms.

Dropping into prone positions, the three others instinctively aimed their rifles in separate directions. Lucas growled at the others, "See anything?"

All answering, "No," Carlos added, "and I didn't hear anything either. Did anyone hear a shot?"

Sparks was peeking out from under his arms. Pointing, he answered, "No, but I saw a flash. It came from the base of the cinder cone, on the right at one o'clock from my position," adding, "under that dark patch."

The three others looked up in the direction Sparks was pointing. Reaching into his pack, Carlos pulled out his high powered binoculars, finding the dark patch and inching his focus downward to the base of the cinder cone. "Are you sure? I can't see anything or anybody."

Defensively, Sparks replied, "I know what I saw. I'm not hallucinating." All four were now looking through their binoculars at the spot and all around it.

Lucas commanded, "Okay, stay low and spread out. Keep your eyes on the spot." Moving quickly, the men separated in a line with five meters in between each of them.

"There it is!" Ropes shouted from the right. "It is not a muzzle flash. It is a reflection off of something shiny, something big."

Feeling vindicated, Sparks moved up beside Ropes. "I see it." Switching through different filters on his binoculars, Sparks said, "It's not moving, and it is not a person. Maybe it is just a shiny rock?" Answering his question, Lucas responded, "According to the map, the trail ends right about there, five hundred meters away."

Taking one more look through his binoculars, Lucas let them dangle from his neck strap. "Ropes and Sparks, head up along the right side. Carlos and I will go up the left. All eyes and ears."

Moving as quickly as they dared, the men reached the spot at the same time. Carlos was the first to speak. Looking at his distorted reflection in the shiny rock, he said, "Uh, Lucas? I think I found something unusual."

Sparks muttered, "I found it first."

Turning toward him, Carlos announced, "By the authority vested in me, I hereby name this, Sparks' rock."

"Uh, Gee thanks, Carlos. You shouldn't have."

"You seem better, Carlos," Ropes observed.

"Nothing like a short stroll in the park to clear one's head."

Ignoring them, Lucas approached the circular rock. Looking at the base, he saw there was a groove leading to the right. "Ropes, help me with this. Let's see if this thing will move. I think we might be able to roll it to the right."

Reaching up to the top edge with his long arms, Ropes began pulling on the rock and was able to make it move a few inches. Lucas got on the left side and began pushing. "It's moving, keep going."

Seeing that there was an opening behind the rock, Carlos and Sparks pointed their rifles into the darkness. Lucas asked, "Ropes, can you hold it open?"

"I think so. Can we jam a rock into the track?" Looking around, Lucas found a large chunk of lava. It was lighter than it looked, but it seemed solid. Jamming it between the edge of mirrored rock and the track, he said, "Try that." Ropes eased up on his grip and the shiny rock rolled back a few inches and stopped, the chunk of lava crunching under the weight.

Carlos had pulled out his flashlight and was aiming it into the hole. "There is a narrow shelf just inside, and then a tunnel that drops downward". Stepping cautiously into the opening, he said, "I can't see the bottom." Picking up a baseball sized chunk of lava, he looked at his watch and rolled the rock into the tunnel. Listening carefully, he heard it bounce and roll for several seconds and then stop.

"It either hit bottom, or there is a long drop off at the end."

Sliding out of his pack, Ropes reached inside and removed his climbing rope. "There is nothing to anchor it up here, so I'll need one of you to be my anchor." Handing one end to Lucas, Ropes tied a safety knot in the other end. Throwing the knotted end down the shaft, he stepped his left leg over the rope, straddling it, with his back toward the shaft. "We may not have time to gear up, so I'll do a dulfersitz rappel. Coms on." He turned his on as the others did the same.

Wrapping the rope between his legs and up around his right hip, he threw it across his chest and over his left shoulder. Holding the anchor side of the rope in his right hand, he grabbed the other side behind him with his left hand and began backing into the shaft. Looking at Lucas, who had wrapped the anchor end around him several times and was now sitting down, with his feet braced against the lip of the entrance, Ropes asked, "On belay?"

"Belay on," Lucas replied.

Leaning back, Ropes slowly disappeared into the shaft. In less than a minute, his voice came over the coms, "Off belay. Piece of cake. You don't need the rope, just slide down the shaft. It should be fun. Let go of your end, Lucas, and everyone come join the party."

One by one, the men launched themselves into the shaft, sliding to the bottom. Carlos couldn't help himself, and let out a long "weeeeeee" on his way down. The shaft ended at a T intersection. Ropes was shining his light down the tunnel to the right and then up the tunnel inclining to the left. "Which way?"

"The map doesn't say, but I'm guessing we go the hard way to the left," Lucas answered. "Any opinions?"

Ropes was now on his knees in the tunnel, shining his light on the floor. "It looks like they went the hard way," pointing up the tunnel to their left. Shining his light at the walls and ceiling, he offered, "This isn't man made. This is a lava tube."

Looking into the darkness, Lucas turned on his flashlight, clipping it to his rifle, and nodded, "The hard way it is. I'll take point."

Carlos was starting to object, when he felt a hand on his arm. Ropes was looking at him and shaking his head slightly. Carlos thought a moment and nodded back in agreement.

Lucas was already moving up the tunnel at a fast pace, the beam from his flashlight making a slow circle from floor to walls to ceiling and back.

"Get up there Sparks," Ropes suggested. "Keep him out of trouble. I'll bring up the rear."

Switching off his flashlight as Sparks passed him, Carlos whispered, "Save your batteries."

Sparks nodded, switching off his light and clipping it to his rifle, he moved to catch up with Lucas, silhouetted by his circle of light.

Following them up the tunnel, Carlos mused, remembering Shakespeare, *Once more unto the breach, dear friends, once more...But when the blast of war blows in our ears, then imitate the actions of a tiger...*

Chapter 18   Saturday Evening. The Mendoza Connection

Jesús was panicking as the room suddenly filled with a deep vibrating tone bouncing off the walls. He hadn't touched the metal box or wire in many minutes. *Why is it vibrating now?* Feeling the vibrations come up through the floor, he wondered if he had set something in motion that he could not stop.

The candle was sitting on the floor in front of the tall metal panel, and the flame seemed to vibrate in concert with the loud tone. The hairs on the back of his neck began to stand up as if the room was becoming electrically charged. Trying to decide whether to stay or to run back down the tunnel, Jesús decided to first pick up the candle before it went out.

As he was standing back up, he saw the panel start to vibrate and change color. Starting as a dull gray, it was now becoming the yellow-orange color of the sun rising up on the horizon. The colors began to swirl, and Jesús realized they were forming an image just like the one engraved on the cover of the old book. It looked like the sun with a spiral in the middle. *Am I supposed to mix the powders and ingest them now?*

Before he could complete that thought, the image started changing again, becoming translucent. Standing transfixed in front of the panel, Jesús realized he could not run. He was feeling pulled by the swirling colors and almost paralyzed by the vibrations that were now resonating inside of his whole body. *Maybe the powders were supposed to protect me from whatever is going to happen next.*

Staring into the panel, Jesús saw the translucent colors disappearing as the panel vibrated into a clear opening, a doorway into another room. It was a mirror image of this room, except for the huge man in a black robe, staring back at him. Jesús saw in his eyes that he was as frightened as he was, except he could sense something malevolent under the surface. *I should have brought the sword. I am defenseless here.*

The man was reaching out toward the panel, and Jesús backed up a step. The man reached the panel and both hands stopped suddenly at the threshold, as if there was a thick glass wall separating the rooms. He began pounding on the clear wall and he seemed to be shouting, and pointing to the edge of the panel, but no words crossed the barrier.

Breathing a sigh of relief, Jesús moved closer to the panel, reaching out and carefully pushing his finger forward until it was stopped by the invisible glass doorway. It was cold and solid, but still vibrating.

Of course; this is the Arca Deus. Putting his face near the opening, he peered into the room and saw that on the other side, at his left, a metal box and tube, just like his own was hanging horizontally out from the edge of the panel.

Looking down at his own box, Jesús began to wonder what would happen if he attached his box to the panel. Setting the candle down in front of the window, he picked up the box, marveling at its lightness, and he examined the end cap of the tube. It was irregular, like the holes under the tiles. *So, this is the key, and the holes are like locks. But which hole does it go into, and what if it opens a doorway between the rooms? I don't trust that man. He looks evil. But maybe it is a distortion caused by the window? Maybe he needs help.*

Picking up the box, Jesús looked at the doorway, but now it was no longer clear and he could not see through it. The colors were swirling like the sun. Hurrying forward, he inserted the end of the tube into what he thought was the same tile as on the other side. Plucking the cable, the tone and vibrations increased in volume and intensity. The colors were swirling and fading once again into transparency. Jesús now heard another sound, screaming, coming from the other room.

Looking back though the window, Jesús was horrified at what he was seeing. Two more people in black robes were now in the room, and one was a woman. Their eyes were deep pockets of blackness and malevolence. The new man had a long knife and he and the woman were now moving toward the huge man and were staring with wary fascination at Jesús through the window.

The big man started running headlong toward the window. Suddenly shots rang out and the new man and woman shuddered and spun around as they were struck by the bullets. The long knife was spinning end over end as it clattered to the floor. One of bullets missed and bounced off the wall behind Jesús. Seeing four new men with rifles running into the room and sliding to a stop, Jesús backed up as he saw one of them taking aim at the big man just as he was leaping through the doorway.

Moving swiftly, Jesús removed the key, but the man was almost all the way through the doorway. The tone and vibrations stopped suddenly and the panel turned dark. The man was screaming as he hit the floor. Part of his foot was sliced off cleanly, the other part presumably still in the other room. Moving backwards in fear, Jesús dropped the box. The man was holding his ankle and rolling on the floor, screaming in pain.

Taking pity on the man and feeling responsible for his pain, Jesús instinctively moved forward and knelt down beside him. "I am so sorry. Let me help you. I might have something for your pain."

Looking up past the man toward the table on which sat his knapsack, Jesús was starting to get up to get it, when he felt a searing pain in his stomach.

Looking down, he saw that the man was pulling a long knife out of his Jesús' body. Jesús' white robe was turning a dark wet red. *No, no. I was trying to help.* Falling backwards, he slowly sank to the floor crumbling into unconsciousness.

Sitting up, Benigno slipped out of his backpack and quickly opened the zippers. Pulling out a short piece of cord and wrapping it around his ankle, he twisted it into a tourniquet to stop the bleeding. Removing a large red plastic box, he found a packet of quik-clot powder, quik-clot bandages, and a bottle of antiseptic.

Examining his foot, he saw he was missing his big toe and parts of the next two toes. The incision was as if a powerful laser had sliced away several inches of his foot and toes in a clean stroke. There wasn't even that much blood, as the wound appeared to be cauterized. Untying the tourniquet did not cause the trickle of bleeding to increase. Pouring the antiseptic over his foot, he screamed in pain for several seconds. Calming himself with the *Cantar Doler*, he then wrapped the bandage around what was left of his foot.

Looking back at the old man, he saw that he was still breathing, and he was still unconscious. Picking up the candle and struggling to get up, Benigno hung on to the metal panel for support, and then hopped over to the table. Quickly sorting through the items, he took what he thought he needed, stuffing them into his pack. Seeing something he previously missed sitting the floor, he pointed his light at it. It was a mess of tangled wires and old vacuum tubes. There were several knobs and dials on a mangled face plate. *It is some kind of radio, he thought. What is it doing here?* Shaking his head, he knew he had to get moving.

Taking one last look at the room, he began to hobble down the tube, leaning on the wall for support.

Benigno knew he had a long road ahead of him, and plenty of time and money to plot his revenge.

He did not yet realize that he was now in Mexico, inside the Pinacate volcano, over 8,000 kilometers away from the *Arca Deus* portal in the Tupungatito volcano.

****

Watching in horror as the huge man in the black robe was running away, Sparks saw him leap through some kind of doorway that suddenly shut, slicing off part of the man's foot. Parts of the man's toes and foot dropped to the floor and bounced. Sparks turned away, vomiting and gagging.

Carlos rushed over to the other two bodies. Lucas ran around the panel, expecting to find Benigno lying there. There was no body and no blood.

"What the fuck. Where did he go? Anybody see him?"

Ropes was covering Carlos as he searched the bodies thoroughly and removed their backpacks.

Looking around, Ropes answered, "He's not here, Lucas."

The two bodies were both moaning and they were still alive, but barely. Slipping out of his own backpack, Carlos removed the special first aid kit that José had created. Using the Quik-Clot powder and bandages, he dressed their bullet holes as best he could, while noticing that one of the individuals was a beautiful woman.

Staring down at her, Ropes asked, "Is that your girlfriend Carlos?"

Examining her face for a few moments, Carlos shook his head, "No. This is a different beautiful woman."

Rolling them over, Carlos fastened their hands behind their backs using thick zip ties. Looking up at Lucas, Carlos asked, "Now what?"

Returning from the far side of the panel, Lucas asked, "Are they going to make it?"

"Their only chance is if we get them to a hospital, and fast."

Ropes grunted, "Then they have no chance. I'm not carrying them out of here."

Lucas was looking around the room, trying to figure out what had just happened. He couldn't explain what happened to Benigno. *How could we lose him? There is no place to go. People don't just disappear into thin air.*

"Listen up," Lucas commanded. "These two have valuable information. Benigno disappeared somehow through that door or whatever it was, and I think these two were planning on taking over. We could take down the whole network with what these two people know."

Looking around the room, Lucas shook his head. "I don't understand what just happened here, and I don't like not knowing. But we can't let any others find out about this place, or about whatever the hell is on the other side of that, uh, door."

Walking over to Sparks, who was now sitting on the floor, holding his head in his hands, Lucas asked, "Sparks, are you good to go?"

"I just want to get out of here, Lucas. I want to go back to José's, crawl into bed with Steffi, and drink myself into a stupor. After that, I don't know what I want to do."

Trying to give him another task to get him out of his head, Lucas said, "One more thing, Sparks. We

241

need to document this for the Director. Take some photos of this room and make sure you get close-ups of that damn door or whatever it is."

Staring down at the two wounded prisoners, Lucas stated his case. "If we can get them a couple of clicks down the mountain, far enough away from here, I can get an air-evac team up here. I will make sure there is enough room on the choppers to take us back to Carlos' truck and drop us off."

"Choppers?" Sparks exclaimed in anger. "If you can get choppers, why the hell did we spend two days hiking to get here?"

"There is no way I could get permission to fly helicopters into this country's airspace to run a mission on their soil. Getting wounded prisoners out of here is another matter. I might be able to convince the Director to make it happen, given the top level intel we could gather."

Standing up, Carlos grunted, "Well, at least they are small and lightweight. It will be a walk in the park."

Glaring at Carlos for a few moments, Ropes shook his head but finally agreed.

Looking up, Sparks added, "Whatever gets me off this mountain the fastest, works for me."

Pulling his sat phone out of his pack, Lucas tried working it, but it would not even turn on. *Crap, It better not be broken. If I cannot get it to work, these two will be dead soon.*

Looking at his watch, he saw that it was not working either. The dial on his wrist compass was spinning around in a circle.

Seeing the room light up in a flash, Lucas turned, seeing Sparks taking photos with a small camera. *At least that works.*

Nodding at the three men, Lucas said, "Okay then. Lay out a couple of tarps and pads, and let's drag them down the tunnel. Bring the foot too. The hard part will be getting these two up the shaft, but we can do it. Ropes, figure it out before we get there. Let's get moving before they die on us."

Chapter 19   Sunday. The Hacienda

Sitting around the table, José, Maria, and the four women were eating in silence. It was almost 11 AM and despite the bright sun outside, the room was filled with a dark gloom. Several times José had tried to make humorous observations, but no one looked up from their plates. Finally, Alícia broke the silence.

"What is going on here, José? They filled us with bullshit about some kind of mission and then they disappear into the morning without any real explanation. What is going on?"

Maria cringed at the profanity, but continued picking at her plate without looking up.

Looking up at Alícia with sad eyes, José shrugged and replied the best he could.

"I wish I could tell you, but you know Lucas. Everything is on a need to know basis. He didn't tell me anything about his plans. Only that they might be gone for a few days."

"But I was gone for years. He said he loves me, but as soon as we are back together, he takes off again." Her eyes were misting with anger and sadness.

"Alícia, I know is that, from deep within my bones, he does love you. He was almost destroyed when you disappeared. But I also know he has a deep love

244

of his country, and that he feels he has to protect her. There is something big that is going on that he must try to stop."

Looking at Maria, he continued, "He is the most honorable man I know. He cannot help himself when he feels that America is threatened. And, that is true for his friends. They will follow him into hell itself, if he thinks that is the right thing to do. They are doing this, whatever it is, for all of you. You must trust them."

Looking at him dubiously, Alícia still felt betrayed. The other women shared her feelings.

Antonia spoke up.

"I know it happened fast, too fast, but think I have fallen in love with Carlos. But there is something very sad and dark inside of him. Sometimes he frightens me, although I know he loves me."

Steffi added. "Sparks is incredibly smart, but he is also like a lost puppy. Why is he even involved with these crazy men?"

The other three women glared at her defensively. Marianna asked, "What, you think he is so special? You think he is better than Ropes?"

Antonia started to speak but she was interrupted by a loud crash as four men burst through the front door, guns drawn and pointed at everyone in the room. The women screamed in fear.

The intruders looked like hardened, intense thugs. Each of them was ugly and menacing with evil smiles on their faces. The biggest one shouted, "Down on the floor; Now!"

Moving down to the floor as he was ordered, José noticed that the man had a tattoo on his neck and a Glock in his hand. *Mierda! I left my gun in the bedroom.*

Moving quickly, the other three men knelt over three of their captives and tied their hands behind their backs with thick zip-ties. Moving on to the other two captives, they repeated tying their hands.

"What do you want?" José shouted.

Walking over to him, the biggest one lashed out with his foot, kicking José in the face. Maria screamed.

"Benigno sends his regards. We have been following you for days. Tell me, where did the four men go?"

José groaned, "What four men?"

The leader kicked him again, this time in the ribs.

"Stop it," Maria begged. "We don't know where they went. They didn't tell us. We were just sitting here asking ourselves the same thing."

Shouting at her, the leader commanded, "Shut up you old witch."

One of the other thugs walked over to the presumed leader and whispered in his ear, "We haven't heard from Benigno in days. All we know is that on Tuesday he was taking some of his damn Brujos up into the mountains for some kind of initiation. He won't be back until tomorrow. Maybe his radio broke."

The leader stared at him in disgust and snarled, "You will be dead tomorrow when he finds out you fell asleep when you were supposed to be following those men."

The thug answered, "Well, at least we got the women. We can use them to set a trap. Maybe the men will come for them and everything will be okay."

Looking down at José, he added, "But we have our orders about this one."

The leader thought for a moment, *I'm not taking the rap for losing those men.*

"Take the women out of here!" demanded the obvious leader.

247

One of the thugs started to reach for Maria.

"No, not that one. She stays here."

Maria stared at him in fear. She could not see José's face.

Roughly pulling the four women up onto their feet, the men shoved and moved their captives outside. Two large SUVs had pulled up to the front of the hacienda. "Get in, now!" the big one demanded.

The four captives reluctantly obeyed. Once in the vehicles, they were blindfolded and strapped into their seats. "No more talking!" someone shouted at them.

Sitting quietly, Antonia began to focus her attention, using all of her remaining senses on what was happening to them, and where they were headed.

Two of the men grabbed several large red plastic jugs from the back of the closest SUV. Running into the house, they returned a few minutes later, empty handed. One of the men scratched a flare into life and threw it inside the front door. Within seconds, the hacienda was on fire.

Hearing the fire roaring and smelling the smoke, Alícia started screaming inside of her mind, *No, no, no! Not again.*

Chapter 20   Sunday.   The Hacienda Revisited

Driving down the road to Mendoza, the four men sat in silence.

Lucas was mentally reviewing his earlier conversation with the Director on the sat phone. Once outside of the volcano, the phone worked perfectly. The Director was able to pull some strings, and, by agreeing to share intel with SAFECONAR, the Argentine Federal Counternarcotics Service, he got Lucas the helicopters he needed. The prisoners were on their way to a secret, secure hospital/interrogation facility somewhere outside of Mendoza. There were some things he could not tell the Director over the phone.

Concentrating on his maniacal driving, Carlos didn't have the time or the energy to think far into his future. He would not bother himself thinking about the past. He tried to picture Antonia's face.

Busying himself with his electronics, Sparks was collating the data from all the cell phones they collected. It was the only way he could block out the horrors of the past few days. He did not know it yet, but he was suffering from PTSD. Lucas knew, and he secretly vowed to get him the help he needed.

Ropes had the unique ability to compartmentalize everything in his life, so that no part could negatively affect any other part. Sitting in the back, he was looking out the window and enjoying the scenery and the wild ride.

Slowing his Land Cruiser, Carlos turned down the dirt road to José's hacienda. Pulled from their thoughts, the men were realizing that they were very hungry; hungry for Maria's food, for tequila, and for their women.

"What the fuck?" Carlos exclaimed. From a few hundred meters out, they could see the hacienda was gone and black smoke was rising into the sky. Gunning the engine, Carlos turned into the driveway on two wheels, speeding down the dirt road to what used to be José and Maria's front yard.

Jumping out of the vehicle with their guns drawn, the men spread out and circled the pile of burnt wood and rubble that used to be the hacienda. The stone foundation and walls were blackened, but still standing proudly amidst the ruins. It was still too hot for them to get close to it. Looking around for any active threats, the four men started running to the casitas that were all still standing untouched.

The men frantically ran to their casitas in unison, bursting through the unlocked doors, guns drawn.

All six casitas were empty, except for the four dresses last worn by their women. The dresses were hanging in the closets. Their purses were in their rooms, but their cell phones were gone.

Lucas found a piece of paper attached to Alícia's dress. Grabbing it as his anger boiled inside his chest, he read the sloppy handwriting.

Go home, gringos. Call this number when you go home to your America and we might set free your friends.

Carlos, Ropes and Sparks were staring at him from outside the door. Carlos spoke up, "What is it?"

Lucas looked up at them with a fierce expression that they had never seen before.

"It is a declaration of war."

End Note

Note from the author:

I hope you enjoyed my first book in the Lucas Forge series.

If you did enjoy it, please take a few moments to rate this book on Amazon/Kindle and write a few sentences about what you liked, so that other readers may find Lucas Forge and his team.

Please check in with me at my blog at:

http://drscottsindelarbooks.blogspot.com
Dr Scott Sindelar Books

Tell your friends, family, and co-workers about this book and read Book 0, The Mendoza Connection: A Prequel, and Book 2 in this series, entitled: The Pinacate Connection, coming summer 2016.

You may also enjoy my short story: The Man Who Would Be Savior, also on Amazon Kindle and Amazon Books:
http://amzn.to/2bwRbcR

Excerpt from Book 2: The Pinacate Connection

Chapter 1   Sunday. The Hacienda, Mendoza, Argentina

Attempting to search the wreckage of the smoldering hacienda, Dr. Lucas Forge, forensic psychologist, and leader of his team of three covert operations specialists were repelled by the intense heat. Pulling the piece of paper from his pocket, Lucas read the note again, trying to find any additional clues.

A few minutes earlier, Lucas had found the piece of paper attached to Alícia Jamison's dress in one of the casitas. Finally reunited with her after three long years, he apparently lost her once again. Running a hand through his sandy brown hair, he glared at the sloppy handwriting.

Go home, gringos. Call this number when you go home to your America and we might set free your friends.

On the back of the note was a telephone number with an Argentine area code. *Did he mean all of our friends, including José and Maria, or just the four women?* Alternating feelings of rage and desperation were battling for domination inside Lucas.

He and his team had been sent here last week to track down the wealthy and ruthless drug lord Don Benigno Sanchez. What they found was that he was also some kind of witch doctor, a Brujo Negro who was the leader of an international cult of Brujo Negros. They practiced some ancient dark art of secret herbs and mental manipulation, and they were controlling politicians and the news media in several countries.

Looking intently at the ground in front of the ruined hacienda, Richard "Ropes" Danzinger and Carlos Cholla were also looking for clues. Ropes was the better tracker of the two, but not by much. Standing awkwardly off to the side, Sheldon Sparks, the tall electronics and pharmaceutical expert, was feeling helpless. Using his brilliant mind, he was able to decipher and track the zeros and ones in computer code, but was still a novice when it came to tracking the patterns left behind by humans or animals.

After many minutes, Ropes looked up toward Lucas and waved him over. Stuffing the paper back into his pocket, Lucas hurried over to the two men.

"What can you tell me?"

"There were three vehicles, probably Suburbans," Ropes said. "One of them has a small oil leak, so it may be an older model. It looks like four or maybe six pairs of footprints entered the hacienda and returned. They were all wearing boots." Moving a few steps over and pointing downward, he added, "Carlos and I think that the four women were pushed and dragged out of the hacienda and placed in one of the vehicles." Lowering his eyes, Ropes continued, "I am sorry, Lucas, but we cannot find any tracks for José or Maria."

As the hot wind shifted, Sparks asked, "What is that weird smell?"

Turning toward Sparks, the three men inhaled in unison. Looking back at Ropes, Lucas recognized the odor as their eyes met. Closing his eyes, Carlos slowly shook his head as he too knew the scent of burnt human flesh. Raising his hands to his face as he looked towards the fiery remains, Sparks cried out, "Oh no." *José and Maria must be buried inside.*

Falling to his knees, Carlos stared at the former home of his old friend. Closing his eyes tightly to force back his tears, he began to pray. "Heavenly Father, I beseech you to watch over the souls of José and Maria Montoya. Please forgive them for their sins and welcome them into your house. We ask this in the name of your son, Jesus Christ." Crossing himself, he looked toward the others, all of whom were standing with bowed heads. Their lips were moving in silent prayers of their own.

Opening his eyes, Lucas' jaw began to pulse with tension. His focus settled into that thousand yard stare as his powerful mind began analyzing the data they accumulated during the last week. Dropping down on one knee, Lucas pulled a small notebook and pen from his left shirt pocket and began writing and drawing diagrams. Sparks started to interrupt him, but Ropes held up his hand, signaling him to stay silent.

Standing up, Carlos pulled a dark blue bandana from his back pocket and wiped it across his face. As he did so, his look of sadness was wiped away and replaced with one of angry determination. Slapping the dirt from his knees, he had one thought. *They are going to pay for this.*

Seeing that Lucas was deep into some analysis, Carlos scanned the property once more for any movement. Finding none, he quietly walked back to his olive green Land Cruiser and opened the rear hatch. One by one, he began organizing their backpacks, dividing up their ammunition and making mental notes of the items that needed to be replaced or refilled.

Hearing footsteps behind him, he spun around, instantly drawing his pistol to the ready position with his trigger finger resting on the slide. Seeing it was Ropes and Sparks, who were now taking a step back with their empty hands raised in submission, Carlos growled, "You know better than to sneak up on me." Slowly re-holstering his pistol, he whispered, "We need to clean the rifles. Let's do them one at a time, so that three of them will always be ready, just in case we need them."

It was starting to get dark, so Carlos flipped on the overhead light, and began to lay out a blanket onto the rear deck of his truck. Handing a rifle to Ropes and another to Sparks who was now next to him, he asked, "Ropes, can you stand guard while I show Sparks how to break these down and clean them?"

Without waiting for a reply, Carlos motioned for Sparks to come closer. Looking at Spark's face in the fading light, he saw that his friend had changed. Sparks had lost his innocence and was fighting a new set of demons inside his mind. Carlos had seen this transformation in many young men over the years. *I hope he makes it through to the other side. Lucas needs to talk to him. All I can do now is to try to keep him busy.*

Speaking slowly to Sparks, he took him step by step through the disassembly and cleaning process and showed him how to reassemble and check the functioning. When he was finished, he told Sparks to repeat the process with his own rifle and took a step back. Carlos repeated the time honored learning method, "See one, do one, teach one." Sparks nodded absently. "Okay, but who the fuck am I going to teach one to?"

Smiling slightly, Carlos replied, "I guess Ropes can be your student tonight." Ropes started to protest, but Carlos silenced him with a hard look. Exhaling, Ropes understood what Carlos was trying to do for

Sparks. "Okay, okay. I could use a refresher
course."

Sparks fumbled a little on the reassembly, but with
a few reminders, he successfully completed the
task. He actually seemed to enjoy teaching the
procedure to Ropes. When they were finished,
Ropes turned to him and said, "Good job, Sparks."
Sparks nodded and turned away. Carlos thought he
saw a slight smile on his face.

"What good job?" Lucas was now standing behind
the men, who jumped at the sound of his voice.
They never heard him coming. Carlos had spun
around again with his hand on the grip of his pistol.
Lucas was too fast, and had placed his own hand
over Carlos'. Grimacing, Carlos warned, "I'm
going to end up shooting one of you guys if you
don't stop sneaking up on me."

Snorting, Ropes gave Sparks a knowing look.
"Don't worry, Carlos. I'll make lots of noise next
time. Maybe you are getting a little rusty."

Ignoring them, Lucas began talking. "I've been
doing some mental debriefing about the last week.
Don Benigno and his thugs seemed to know where
we were and a lot about what we were doing. They
ambushed us on the trail and they found the
hacienda. They knew about José and probably knew
about the women. Either one of them was playing
both sides, or somehow the hacienda was bugged."

Jumping in, Sparks said, "Maybe they bugged our gear?"

"That's a possibility. Can you check it out, Sparks?"

Sparks replied, "I'll see what I can do," and he began going through his bag of electronics. The sun had set long ago, but the moon was rising from the east.

Turning toward Ropes and Carlos, Lucas continued, "The hacienda had to be burning for hours, and yet no one has come out to check; there have been no fire trucks, no Federales, not even a neighbor. I can think of only a few explanations; they have been bought off, they are somehow involved, or maybe they are afraid of Don Benigno and his minions. We've seen some of what they can do with their mind tricks and with their drugs. We still don't know how Benigno escaped. We had him in that lava tube, and then he suddenly disappeared. He had to have help. Something or someone got him out of there."

Staring angrily into Lucas' eyes, Carlos asked, "You're not suggesting that José is, I mean, was a traitor, are you?"

"I'm not suggesting, I'm asking. You knew him the best and for the longest time. You knew his history. He was no Boy Scout. And this property did not come cheap. Do you really think he could've

259

afforded this place with the money he made from
his store in Mendoza?"

Looking down at his feet, Carlos replied, "Well,
no." Looking back up, he added, "But I guess I just
assumed he made his money a long time ago, before
he and Maria moved here."

Studying Carlos' face, Lucas noticed that one side
was illuminated by the rising moon, and had a
grayish tint, while the other side looked orange
from the glow of the still smoldering hacienda. It
was as if Carlos had two different faces. Lucas was
struggling inside of his mind. He knew he could
trust Carlos with his life, but the events of the last
week had unnerved him.

Thinking back, he remembered thinking that Carlos
had been eager to kill the man from the airport. He
also kept telling Lucas to forget about Alícia
Jamison, and that she was nowhere to be found.
Then suddenly, she shows up at the hacienda after
supposedly spending years in captivity by
Benigno's men. *Why now? And how did José find
her?* Then, on the trail to Tupungatito, he found
Carlos supposedly passed out after being
hypnotized or drugged by a Bruja Negra.

Lucas did not believe in coincidences. He was
trained to look for patterns in seemingly disparate
data. Knowing the complexities of the human mind
and the fragile human motivations that could be

easily manipulated, trust in others was something that did not come easily to him. Having betrayed many others in his life, he had also been on the receiving end of numerous betrayals. Knowing Carlos for a long time, he had watched with sadness as Carlos left behind a long trail of betrayed women and their broken hearts.

Lucas was often guided by the words of President Ronald Reagan. When the president was negotiating mutual nuclear disarmament with the Soviet Union, he lived by the motto "Trust, but verify."

Lucas thought he had verified his trust in Carlos many years ago, and was disturbed by his now emerging doubts. He knew it was important to be aware of his own feelings and instincts, but to never trust them without verification, especially in matters of life and death, and in matters of the heart.

Lucas decided that he now would have to watch Carlos carefully. *This is going to be a dangerous distraction.*

"Lucas, I found something!" Sparks shouted. He appeared to be holding something in his upraised hand. He was wearing a headlamp, and the glow from it cast eerie shadows on his face.

As Lucas approached him, Sparks added, "Actually, I found two devices. One is a miniature transmitter that I found inside the butt stock of one of the rifles.

The second was a larger transmitter hidden behind
the glove box in Carlos truck."

Lucas was staring at the objects in Spark' hands, but
he was thinking about Carlos. The devices were in
Carlos' truck and in one of the rifles he obtained
from José. Spark's continued, "Lucas, someone has
been tracking us all along."

THE MENDOZA CONNECTION

About the Author

Photo Credit: Susan Carroll Sindelar

As a clinical psychologist, neuropsychologist, and forensic psychologist, Dr. Scott Sindelar has been assisting patients and clients for over 30 years. He taught in the psychology department at Arizona State University, designed and managed inpatient and residential dual-diagnosis (Substance Abuse + Other Psychological Disorders) programs, and has a private practice in Scottsdale, AZ.

He enjoys writing, teaching, and helping a larger audience through seminars and writing than he could ever reach through his private practice.

He is also a Trike pilot, flying motor gliders (a safe and enjoyable sport, as seen in the movie Fly Away

Home). He can be seen flying his own Trike in scenes from the film The Hoax, by Walker O'Brien.

As an avid reader, he has noticed that the volume of books he reads has increased dramatically since obtaining a Kindle and syncing it with his iPhone and laptop.

Dr. Sindelar shares a home with his best friend and wife, Susan, and the best dog in the world, Pippin.

www.ingramcontent.com/pod-product-compliance
Lightning Source LLC
Chambersburg PA
CBHW070800200626
46811CB00023B/304

* 9 7 8 1 8 8 8 7 7 4 0 7 8 *